IDENTITY

Other titles by Sandra Glover

IDENTITY

SANDRA GLOVER

ANDERSEN PRESS LONDON

First published in 2010 by
ANDERSEN PRESS LIMITED
20 Vauxhall Bridge Road, London SW1V 2SA
www.andersenpress.co.uk
www.sandraglover.co.uk

British Library Cataloguing in Publication Data available.

ISBN 978 184 270 993 1

Typeset in Sabon by Palimpsest Book Production Limited,
Grangemouth, Stirlingshire
Printed and bound in Great Britain by CPI Bookmarque,
Croydon CR0 4TD

For Mike, with love.

Prologue

She jogged along the path, listening to her music, keeping her pace steady. It was drizzling and there was a light mist but she didn't mind the weather or the fact that the park was quiet, totally deserted at that time in the morning. What she did mind was the growing feeling that the park wasn't quite as deserted as it seemed, that there was someone else around, watching her.

Pausing for a moment, she pulled at a strand of hair that was flopping round her face and tucked it behind her ear. She looked around. There was no one there. So why was she so sure she wasn't alone? She shivered, then set off again, quickening her pace but keeping to her familiar route. It wouldn't be long now before she reached the gates, out onto the road and home.

She kept alert, kept looking right and left. She even glanced behind. No one was following but, as she turned back a man, a youngish man, stepped out from behind one of the trees, right in front of her, forcing her to stop. Blue jeans, black top, cap, thin face, long nose; that was all she had time to take in before she saw the knife.

Close, he was far too close. She couldn't turn, couldn't run, her mind, her limbs had seized up. His arm, the knife, the smooth, sharp, pointed blade were already flashing towards her.

1

'Are we nearly there yet?' Louise asked. 'We've used up a month's petrol ration already.'

Her father turned round, peering at her through the gap between the headrests.

'That's a bit of an exaggeration,' he said. 'Anyway, it's not far now. We get off the motorway at Derby.'

Ah, clue at last! Derby, it was somewhere near Derby this time. Louise paused the film she'd been half-watching, in a useless attempt to relax, to take her mind off things, and glanced out of the window, hoping to see a sign, something to tell her exactly where they were now.

'It's about another ten miles or so,' her father said.

Another ten miles could take all day, the speed her mother was driving. Talk about careful, it was ridiculous! The motorway wasn't busy, which was one good thing about the petrol rationing, but still Mummy pootled along in the inside lane, way below the speed limit in typical oldie style! Even lorries had passed them. The only thing that hadn't caught up was that funny-shaped little blue car, a mile or so back.

'I don't see why we have to go at all,' Louise said.

'Don't start all that again, Louise,' her father said. 'It's only once a year, now. One day out of your summer holiday. It's not too much to ask, is it?'

'But I don't like it. It's stupid, I don't want to go. I don't like *her*!'

'Why?' he said. 'She doesn't hurt you, does she?'

Well no, there was only one bit that actually hurt, then only for a moment, but that wasn't the point.

'It's only a check-up,' he added when she didn't answer him.

'But I don't need a check-up, do I? I'm fine. Look at me, do I look sick? I play volleyball for the school and swim for the county. I'm not too thin or too fat. I haven't had so much as a cold for the past five years and please don't start giving me all that crap about being premature.'

'Louise!' said her mother. 'We don't spend all that money on your education for you to use words like that.'

Louise groaned. What world, what century were her parents living in if they thought crap was a rude word or that no one in private schools ever swore? She knew the answer, of course. It wasn't just that her parents were seriously old-fashioned, they were seriously old! They were old enough to be her grandparents; a complete and total embarrassment. They'd have been happier back in the middle of the twentieth century, when they were born, rather than well into the twenty-first.

'It is though,' Louise insisted, 'it's rubbish. Naomi's sister was a seriously premature baby. She was in intensive care for six weeks but she doesn't have to have stupid check-ups every year.'

'You haven't been talking to your friends about this, have you?' her father asked, his voice sounding suddenly croaky, hoarse.

'No, but I don't know why it has to be a secret.'

'It's not a secret, exactly,' her mother said, 'it's just not something we talk about. It's private, personal. We've been though all this, Louise.'

'Yes, I know,' Louise said, slumping back in her seat.

They sure had! They'd been telling her the same story since she'd been old enough to ask. How her mother had been a 'career woman', how she'd never wanted marriage or kids until she'd met Daddy and by that time they'd left it a bit late. Her mother was thirty-nine and Daddy was forty-two. Not exactly geriatric and pregnancy was definitely still possible, only it didn't happen, did it?

They'd told her all the gory details. How they'd had fertility treatment without success. How, by the time her mother was forty-seven, they'd virtually given up until they'd found a private clinic offering a revolutionary new treatment for older couples. How there'd been complications at birth. Well, so what? OK, so it was a bit yucky to think she'd started life in a test tube, or whatever they used, and a bit scary to think she almost hadn't made it but she'd survived! She was fine now.

'I can understand why I had to go when I was little,' Louise said, 'but I'm sixteen for heaven's sake. I'm not going to suddenly keel over and die, am I?'

'No, of course not,' her mother said, 'that's not the point. We signed up until you were eighteen.'

'What do you mean, you signed up? You never mentioned that before.'

'It's nothing,' her father said, a little too quickly.

6

'We didn't actually sign anything, as such. It was part of the deal, that's all, in return for their help. They wanted to study children born to older parents as a result of the treatment. So it's really more to do with the big picture, than you personally.'

'I don't care,' said Louise, aware she was sounding 'difficult', as her mother would say. 'I don't want to be part of a picture, big or not. You might have signed up but I didn't, did I? No one asked me.'

'You were a bit young at the time.'

'Well, I'm not now.'

'Please don't make a fuss, Louise,' her mother said. 'I've got a headache.'

Oh right, the famous headaches that came on the minute Mummy didn't want to talk about something!

'Was it legal?' Louise asked.

'What?' said her father.

'The treatment you had, was it legal?' Louise asked again.

'Of course it was legal,' he snapped. 'It wasn't available on the NHS, we had to pay, but it was worth it and there was nothing illegal about it. Honestly, Louise, I don't know where you get your ideas from sometimes.'

Maybe not, maybe she was 'being fanciful' as Daddy called it but there was something wrong with all this, something they'd never told her; some reason, other than Mummy's obsession with privacy, why they wanted it all kept quiet. These weren't ordinary check-ups. They lasted all flaming day for a start. Their appointment was for ten o'clock, as always, and they rarely got away before five. When she'd been younger there'd been more check-ups; mini ones in between the annual marathon. They'd gradually cut back until they were down to just the one but it was unnerving enough.

Louise shivered even though the sun was shining, even though she'd been too hot a second ago. Best not to question it, best just to accept it, like she'd done when she was younger, but there was something new niggling at her, something she'd been wanting to ask for a couple of days but hadn't quite plucked up the courage.

'Is it something genetic?'

She saw her father twitch, as if she'd stabbed him between the shoulder blades. He turned to face her again, more slowly this time.

'What do you mean?'

'You know – some genetic illness in the family, something that gets passed on.'

'Oh, you mean like haemophilia or a weak heart or something,' he said, sounding genuinely relieved.

'No, it's nothing like that. You know what it's about!'

'Yes but I meant more like – mental illness,' Louise said.

Her father shook his head, pushed his glasses up a bit and smiled.

'I really, really don't know where you get your ideas from, Louise.'

'I was thinking of Great-Aunt Mary.'

There, it was out, she'd said it.

'Oh,' he said, 'well, I don't think Aunt Mary's ill as such. I wouldn't say she had a mental illness. She's just a bit eccentric.'

A bit eccentric! Her mother's Aunt Mary had been seriously loopy, totally paranoid, for as long as Louise could remember and she was getting worse. Last week she'd claimed Mummy was an impostor and the week before she'd accused the postman of burying dogs in her garden. How sane was that?

'And I'm sure it's not genetic,' her mother chipped in.

Not that they'd really know. Great-Aunt Mary wouldn't ever see a doctor. She didn't trust doctors and, of course, she didn't think there was anything wrong with her.

'Anyway,' said her father, 'what's set you off thinking about Aunt Mary?'

Louise shrugged. She wasn't going to tell them, no way. Besides it was probably nothing. She was just stressed that's all, more worked-up than usual with exams and the nightmares kicking off again, big time – not to mention this dreaded annual visit to Dr Jay. And it had only happened in the last couple of days; the freaky feeling that someone was watching her. It happened all the time in the nightmares, of course, but she hadn't been asleep on Monday when she was doing her early morning swim at the new super-pool and felt someone watching her from the balcony. She'd ignored it for a while, telling herself it was imagination, but eventually she'd stopped at the end of the pool, taken her goggles off, looked up and found the balcony was as deserted as it always was at that time in the morning.

She hadn't thought too much about it but then yesterday afternoon, when she'd been walking back from Gina's, she'd thought someone was following her. She hadn't seen anybody suspicious or heard footsteps or anything like that; it was just a feeling.

Was that how it started, the paranoia? Would she be digging in the garden looking for dead dogs by this time next week?

'What are you laughing at, Louise?' her mother said, as she finally turned off the motorway.

'Oh, nothing,' Louise said.

She dismissed the mental image of her and Great-Aunt Mary scrabbling around in the soil, looking for dead dogs. It was silly. She wasn't going mad; there was nothing wrong with her mind, absolutely nothing. She just had a vivid imagination, that's all. It was something that had cropped up on all her school reports since nursery.

'Louise is a sensitive child who displays a vivid imagination.'

It was a good thing, wasn't it? She'd always got top marks for her stories, her art and her music. But then she got top marks for most things. She'd even been predicted A grades in science and you couldn't exactly use your imagination in chemistry but it was useful for most things if you kept it under control.

'Don't let your imagination run away with you,' her mother was always saying, especially after Louise had woken them in the middle of the night with her screams, her nightmares. Was that what she was doing now – letting her imagination run wild – with the knot tightening in her stomach, the pressure building behind her eyes? The check-up was nothing to be scared of, nothing to get keyed up about. Daddy was right. She seriously needed to calm down.

They'd left the motorway but they weren't heading towards the city, they never did. The appointments were never in cities or towns. They were always in out of the way places and never in the same place twice. The day of the week was always the same, always a Wednesday, but always in a different isolated spot. You didn't exactly need much of an imagination to think that was weird. Except her parents seemed to think it was perfectly normal, perfectly reasonable.

'Dr Jay's based abroad,' her parents had said, the first time Louise had asked a few years ago. 'She just rents a place for a few weeks each summer, somewhere peaceful so she can combine it with a bit of a holiday at the same time.'

OK, so there was nothing wrong with that. Why shouldn't Dr Jay spend her summers in little holiday cottages halfway up mountains or in the middle of the moors? This was neither mountain nor moor but they'd already left the main road and were heading off into the countryside. Louise kept watching, left, right, out of the back window, trying to keep track of where they were although she wasn't sure why. The Nav system, with its flash live-view upgrades and info about all the latest toll charges which seemed to increase every day, was switched off, as it always was for these journeys, and her parents weren't even using a map, as though they'd memorized the route and swallowed the evidence!

Louise looked out of the back window again, as her mother turned left. That was strange. The small blue car that had been behind them on the motorway, travelling every bit as slowly as they'd been, was still there. Were they being followed? No, stop it! There was no one watching, no one following, it was crazy. Why did she get so hyped-up about all this, what did it matter? So Dr Jay was a bit weird, a bit creepy, but it would all be over soon and by tonight she'd be back home, safe in Harrogate. And it wasn't like she was on her own. Her parents were with her. They'd never let anything bad happen to her. Nothing bad had ever happened before – either on the fifteen other Wednesdays in the summer holidays, when she'd seen Dr Jay, or during any of the old mini-checks in between – so why did she hate it so much?

She closed her eyes, squeezing them tight shut. Don't look, don't think about it, stop worrying about Dr Jay and tests and blue cars! It probably wasn't even the same blue car she'd seen on the motorway. If someone was following, her mother would have noticed and why should anyone follow them anyway? Why would anyone waste their petrol? What the hell was wrong with her today?

With her eyes shut, the twists, turns and jolts on the road were making her feel sick and after ten minutes or so she couldn't stand it. She opened her eyes, reached into her bag and took out a bottle of sparkling water she'd bought at the services. It tasted flat and warm but it was better than nothing. They were on a very narrow, winding lane now. Louise risked a glimpse out of the back. There was no blue car and when she turned round again they'd arrived. The lane had come to a halt at the start of a small wood, and set back from the road was a cottage.

There was no garage and no car parked outside. Dr Jay never seemed to have a car with her. She probably came by train and got a bi-kab from the station. The eco-friendly way to travel! Or maybe

Dr Jay just materialized through some sort of portal, some other dimension. Nothing would surprise her about Dr Jay.

Louise got out of the car and stretched as her parents got their stuff out of the boot. They'd barely set foot on the short path when the cottage door opened. Dr Jay never looked much different. She must be in her fifties now but her hair was still sleek, glossy brown, cut short in the same style as last year and the year before. Skin stretched over high cheek bones with barely a wrinkle. Had she had surgery, collagen or what?

Possibly, almost everyone of a 'certain age' did, including Louise's parents, but then Dr Jay had always looked a bit false somehow with her plastic smile, unnaturally white teeth and those eyes! Deep, leafy green, like she'd had colour enhancement or was wearing coloured lenses. Maybe there was nothing real about Dr Jay, not even her name. Louise had tried looking her up on line but although there were loads of Dr Jays, none was her Dr Jay and even refined searches hadn't got her anywhere. So maybe she was right about portals and dimensions. Dr Jay was an alien and 'abroad' was some far-off galaxy!

'Come in,' Dr Jay said, like it was an order rather than an invitation.

They went through into a small sitting room. Everyone knew the routine. Her parents were already sitting down, preparing to work. They'd both officially retired a few years ago but they still 'dabbled', as they put it, doing media consultancy work, running the occasional training day. Dr Jay asked a few polite questions about how they were but it wasn't them she was interested in and within seconds she was leading Louise upstairs.

Now this really was like stepping through a portal, no imagination required – from quaint country cottage downstairs, to high-tech clinic upstairs. Both bedrooms were packed with machines. There was nothing else, no wardrobes, no furniture unless you counted the office chairs, the small desk and the bed, which wasn't the kind you slept in, it was the kind you were examined on. As she followed Dr Jay into the room with the bed, Louise automatically pulled a band from her pocket, scraped her hair back from her face and twisted it into a high ponytail. Hair had to be tied back. She also stepped onto the scales without being asked. Weighing was always first.

'OK, good,' said Dr Jay, as Louise's weight registered on-screen.

That was the easy bit. Next came the measuring,

not just her height but the length of her fingers, the distance between her eyes, the length of her nose. Why did they need to know this stuff? What had the length of her nose or the width of her big toenail got to do with anything? All the time, Dr Jay was watching her, her face impassive, her eyes hard, as if she'd deliberately closed part of herself down. If there was ever any emotion there to close off, of course. There wasn't much conversation, there never was, at this stage. The 'little talk' came later. For now it was all 'that seems fine, Louise' and 'just pop up on the bed, for me, can you?' As Louise stretched out on the bed, a memory came out of nowhere; a memory of a man, an older man, even older than her parents and Dr Jay.

'There used to be someone else, didn't there?' she asked. 'Another doctor with you, a man?'

'Oh, yes, gosh,' said Dr Jay. 'Fancy you remembering that. He came once or twice but he, er, retired, many years ago.'

She said the last few words so abruptly you could almost hear the full stop clicking in at the end of the sentence – conversation over, terminated. Dr Jay briskly got on with the business of the blood pressure, the temperature, then the bit Louise hated: the blood tests. Needles, she really, really hated needles or anything sharp, pointed, metallic. She could feel herself tense as Dr Jay raised the vein.

'It's all right, Katherine,' Dr Jay said, 'just relax.'

Katherine, who the hell was Katherine? Her last victim probably! Dr Jay didn't seem to notice her mistake, why should she, she probably got through dozens of her little 'guinea pigs' in the week or so she spent on earth!

'So how many of us are there? Owww! Bloody hell!'

'Sorry,' Dr Jay said, 'the needle slipped. Sorry. I'll just – that's better. Sorry about that, Louise.'

So they were back to Louise now. Louise closed her eyes, tried to take deep breaths, waited until the blood was taken and the needle safely out of the way before she asked again.

'So how many of us are there?'

'What do you mean, how many?' Dr Jay said.

'Children of older parents,' said Louise, 'taking part in these trials or whatever they are.'

'Oh, yes, of course. Well, quite a lot. Yes, we need a reasonably large sample.'

Quite a lot, a reasonably large sample, what sort of answer was that from a scientist? Not exactly precise and Dr Jay seemed really tense, distracted today, not her usual efficient self.

'So what's going to happen to all the information?'

'Goodness,' said Dr Jay. 'You are asking a lot of questions today, Louise! Well, we collate it all into charts, look for patterns and if we find anything interesting no doubt we'll publish it.'

'And who's we? Who do you work for?'

'A consortium of private clinics, I'm sure your parents have told you. You can pop off the bed now. We'll go next door and you can do a few little tests for me.'

This section had come a bit sooner than usual. It was probably Dr Jay's way of shutting her up, plonking her in front of a screen to answer questions, look at pictures and play games. First up was spelling. When she was little she'd been given pictures and had to write in the words: *rabbit, table, umbrella*. She remembered the old man, the other doctor, had been dead impressed with umbrella. How old had she been then, five, maybe six? Strange thing to remember but the older doctor had been sort of nice, more human than alien, and it had all seemed like fun back then.

Now it was picking out the right spelling: *occassionally, ocassionally, occasionally*. She thought about deliberately getting it wrong, mucking up their results but there was no point. She sighed. She'd never make a rebel! She'd been moaning and fretting about all this for the past five years or so but she always conformed in the end.

Halfway through, her mother brought tea and biscuits but she didn't stay. Dr Jay wandered in now and again to see how she was doing and sometimes Louise could sense her in the doorway, watching, but mainly she was left alone. God it was boring, worse than school! Much worse; at least in school she had her friends. She was almost relieved when it was time for lunch and their 'little talk'. Her father delivered cheese sandwiches and some fruit, leaving her to eat it with Dr Jay.

'So, Louise,' said Dr Jay. 'How've you been getting on at school?'

She was obviously trying to sound relaxed, chatty, but it was hardly informal with every word they said appearing on the computer screen and Dr Jay sitting there, plate of sandwiches balanced on her knees, waiting to tap in alterations when the voice recognition got it wrong.

'Fine,' Louise said.

She knew more was required so she rattled off the exams she'd taken, the triumphs of the volley-ball team and the fact that she'd won the Year 11

Poetry Prize. She got the feeling that Dr Jay knew most of this stuff already so did her parents feed her information throughout the year or was Dr Jay just doing some weird little alien mind-probe? Louise shook her head slightly. She ought to give up on this alien thing or she'd start believing it; start seeing funny green men like poor Great-Aunt Mary did sometimes! The chat passed on from school, through to hobbies, friends and embarrassing questions about boyfriends, which she had to confess to a distinct absence of, then, just as Louise was about to bite her apple, a change of focus.

'So have you had any more nightmares?'

No point lying, Dr Jay probably knew already.

'A few, they started again when I was doing exams.'

'And can you remember what they were about?'

'No, I've told you. I never remember.'

It wasn't true. She did remember, all too clearly, but she'd never told anybody, not even her parents. She couldn't, somehow; as if talking about it would make it worse, if that was possible. Her chest was tightening and her hands were going clammy just thinking about it. And, besides, it was sort of nice to think there was something she could keep private.

They couldn't get that deep inside her head. They couldn't pry into her dreams.

'And how frequent have they been?'

Before Louise could answer Dr Jay's wrist-com beeped. Hardly alien technology but it was one of the ultra-slim, flesh-coloured, top-of-the-range, mega-expensive i-com models that seemed to blend into the arm, not a clunky bangle type like hers, which had cost enough! Dr Jay got up and walked towards the window to answer it. Was it to get a better signal or so that Louise wouldn't see? There was a slight change of expression as Dr Jay read the message and tapped in her reply. Obviously it wasn't good news. The com bleeped again and again as messages were exchanged. Dr Jay's face had slipped back into impassive mode but Louise could tell she wasn't pleased.

'Mmm,' Dr Jay said at last, 'something's come up. I'm afraid we'll have to cut our session short. There's someone I need to see, I'm sorry.'

Sorry! It was the best news Louise had heard all week. She pulled the band from her hair and shook her head, letting the hair fall round her shoulders. As she looked up Dr Jay was staring at her, almost transfixed, her too-green eyes shiny and slightly moist.

22

'Is something wrong?' Louise said.

'Wrong – er – no. I was just looking at your hair, Louise. It's lovely, really natural.'

Meaning Dr Jay's wasn't? Did she wear a wig to cover her alien baldness?

'Can I go now?'

'Yes, of course. Goodbye, Louise.'

Maybe it was her imagination again but it sounded as if there was something final in the word 'goodbye'. As though Dr Jay had suddenly decided that there wouldn't be an appointment next year.

2

Sol glanced behind as he pushed open the door to the cellar but there was no sign of the doctor, no sign of anyone following. He almost dropped the torch as the smell invaded his nostrils, his mouth, his throat, making him retch; a damp, musty smell of death and decay. He stepped back.

'Sol?' a faint voice called out. 'Help me.'

It was her – or at least someone, something that sounded like her. He had to do it, he had to find out. Slowly he moved forwards, making his way down the slippery, uneven steps, keeping the beam of the torch shining straight ahead, not daring to look at the steps, to see what was causing the slipperiness.

He tried not to breathe, to take in the smell. At the bottom of the steps there was another door, the same green door he remembered from his dreams. He stretched out his left hand and touched the door, which creaked open. In the dreams it ended here, outside the door but this was no dream; not this time.

'Sol, help me, Sol.'

He stepped inside the dark room with its damp walls and low ceiling. Empty, the room was empty. But no, a slight movement made him shine his torch into the far corner.

'Ellie?' he said. 'Oh God, no!'

Jessica shivered, snapped the book shut and put it on her bedside table as her com rang.

'Oh hi, Kaleem.'

God he was keen! They'd been exchanging texts and e-mails nearly all night. She'd thought he'd be asleep by now.

'You still awake?' he asked.

'No, I always talk in my sleep.'

Kal laughed. That lovely tinkling laugh he had.

'Sorry, yeah, daft question,' he muttered. 'What you doing then?'

'Scaring myself half to death reading,' she said, glancing at the cover of her book. 'All zombies, freaky doctors, dark cellars and creepy graveyards. It's dead good but not what you'd call the best choice for midnight, when I'm home alone.'

'Didn't think you were the type to get spooked by that sort of thing, Jess.'

'I'm not,' she said, hoping he wouldn't think her a total wimp, 'not really. They're all the same, aren't they? I mean, I know exactly what'll happen next. The cellar door's gonna slam shut and this guy Sol's gonna drop his torch and be stuck with mutant-zombie-girl gibbering in the corner.'

'Who used to be his girlfriend, right?'

'Yeah, have you read it?'

'No but like you said it's not hard to guess!'

'So would you come and rescue *me* if I got attacked by a freaky doctor and turned into a zombie?'

'Not sure,' said Kal.

'Oh thanks!'

'I'd probably do something,' said Kal, as if he was seriously considering the possibilities, 'just nothing too heroic. I mean it's just mad what people do in stories, innit? Like they always open their doors when they've been told there's some maniac with a machete on the loose! Don't they think to check?'

'Or they go off into forests at night and start creeping round graveyards,' Jessica said. 'Talk about brainless! Why don't they just call the police?'

'Er – 'cos it wouldn't make much of a story, I guess,' said Kal.

'Suppose so – but you didn't just phone to chat about horror-lit, did you?'

'Didn't phone for anything really. I just like talking to you. I'm sick of being stuck up't north on my own,' he said, in a terrible imitation of a Lancashire accent. 'What a way to spend the hols!'

'You're not on your own,' Jessica pointed out, 'your whole family's there and you've only been gone two days.'

'Don't know why I had to go at all.'

'Duh! Your brother's getting married, remember?'

'Yeah, but it doesn't take a whole flaming week, does it?'

'Stop moaning – you'll love it!'

'I guess – look I'd better go, almost out of credit. Miss you.'

'Miss you too.'

Jessica was surprised to find that she meant it. She'd only been with Kal six weeks and three days although they'd known each other longer – since Kal joined their school in Year 9. She lay there thinking about him for a while, wondering why it had taken them so long to get together, then glanced at the time. It was nearly half twelve and Mum still wasn't back. She turned on her TV, changing channels, checking her stored favourites looking for something light or funny to watch.

OK, it was silly, she knew that but no way could she sleep until Mum got back, even though she was completely shattered after stacking supermarket shelves for the past four days. She unclipped her com from her wrist but before she could put it down on the bedside table, it rang. The sudden lurch of her stomach, the fear that it was Mum, that something was wrong, evaporated when she realized it was Kaleem again.

'I'm still missing you,' he said.

'I thought you were out of credit!'

'I topped up.'

'Good,' she said, 'but we can't talk all night.'

'Why not?'

'Well, Mum will be back soon, for a start, wanting to tell me all about her wild night out with Jonathon. I thought she'd be back ages ago. They've only gone for a meal. I mean how long can it take to eat dinner?'

'Hey, quit panicking – you're starting to sound like my mother. *How can it take you half an hour to walk home, Kaleem? Why didn't you call me? You're the daughter not the parent, Jess!*'

'I know and I'm not panicking,' Jessica insisted,

smiling at Kaleem's impersonation of his mum. 'It's just that Mum doesn't usually stay out this late, 'specially not mid-week.'

'Why don't you ring her if you're worried?'

'I'm not worried!'

Kaleem laughed and she could picture him, head tilted back slightly, his mega-gorgeous dark eyes all shiny and alert.

'Well go to sleep then,' he said.

'I can't, someone keeps phoning me!'

'Whoops, sorry!'

'No, it's OK. I'm not at work again till Sunday, I can have a lie-in tomorrow, if I want, but I bet you can't.'

'No – we'll probably be trying on wedding clothes for the hundredth time or checking guest lists or something dead exciting. So I suppose I'd better get some sleep – if you're sure you're gonna be all right. You can phone me back if your mum doesn't turn up though – if you get worried.'

'No, I'm fine, honest, now go!'

'OK, talk tomorrow, then,' he said.

She looked at her com as the call ended, wondering if she should phone Mum. No, she didn't want to harass her, she'd give her another ten minutes or so. Mum was probably fine and so was she. She didn't really mind being home alone. Like Kal said earlier, she didn't get spooked easily. She wasn't a kid, she was sixteen – she could look after herself. All the doors and windows were locked. She'd checked – twice.

Anyway, at the first hint of any strange noise, any trouble, she'd call the police, Mum, Kal, the neighbours, the SAS, Fire Brigade; all of them, whatever it took. Not like Sol. God, what a total idiot! He'd be OK, though. He was the hero and heroes always got out alive. Maybe she could just read the next bit to see how he escaped from the cellar, as he surely would.

The sound of voices outside saved her the trouble of deciding. She couldn't catch what Mum and Jonathon were saying but she heard Jonathon walking away. He obviously wasn't staying tonight then. She turned off the TV but left the bedside mini-bulb on and slithered down in the bed a bit, as if she'd been dozing. No point letting Mum know she'd been worried about her.

Jessica listened to the sounds, tracing Mum's movements; the tap of heels on the short path, the click of the key, the front door opening and closing then footsteps coming upstairs. If this was a novel, it wouldn't be Mum at all, of course. It would be the mad scientist brandishing an over-large hypodermic. Fictional scientists were nearly always mad, never the heroes, like in real life. Writers really had it in for scientists, which was a bit unfair 'cos people would still be living in mud huts and dying off at thirty-five if it wasn't for science!

Mercifully though this wasn't a story and when the bedroom door opened there was no stereotype doctor with wild, white hair and in a white coat. No, it was just Mum looking flushed, her light brown eyes unusually bright. She'd been drinking. Probably not a lot because it only took a couple of glasses to get Mum tipsy.

'And what time do you call this?' Jessica said in a mock-stern voice, setting Mum off giggling, as she'd known it would. 'I guess you had a good time.'

'Mmm,' said Mum, sitting on the edge of the bed, 'what about you?'

'Been chatting to Kal but I spent most of the night with a crazy scientist, who resurrects dead girls who've got boyfriends with more balls than brains,' said Jessica.

She pointed to the book in case Mum thought she'd really been hanging out with mad scientists and dead people. The state Mum was in, anything was possible and she *had* suddenly gone pale!

'If you're going to throw up,' said Jessica, 'would you mind not using my floor?'

'I'm not, I'm fine,' Mum insisted. 'I'm not drunk.'

Mum picked up the book, looking at the cover and the blurb.

'Uggh,' she said, 'I don't know why you read stuff like that, Jessica. I mean, it's just trash, rubbish. I'm surprised you don't have nightmares.'

Jessica shrugged. OK so the darker stories got to her a bit sometimes but they never affected her sleep. She'd always been a deep sleeper. Once she was off, that was it. Her eyes were starting to close now. Maybe she was even more tired than she'd thought but Mum showed no sign of leaving.

'Jess-ic-a,' Mum said, drawing the name out slowly, 'can I ask you something?'

'Sure,' said Jessica, forcing her eyes open.

'How would you feel if me and Jonathon got married?'

Jessica's eyes were wide now, the tiredness instantly forgotten. Married! Oh, right, so that was what it was all about, that's why Mum had been out so late! Jonathon had poured half a bottle of champagne down Mum's throat and proposed. She glanced at Mum's hand. There was no engagement ring – good. Hopefully that meant nothing was settled – Mum was still thinking about it and was really asking for her blessing first.

'Jessie?' Mum said, her voice almost pleading.

'Er, fine,' said Jessica, trying not to launch in with a whole load of negatives. 'Yeah, I mean I'd be OK with it.'

'You do like Jonathon, don't you?' Mum asked.

''Course I do. What's not to like?'

It was true. Jonathon was nice, pleasant, friendly, steady and very generous. Mum had been seeing him for a couple of years. It wasn't like it was sudden or completely unexpected. Only she'd never thought it was quite so serious, somehow. She really hadn't seen this coming.

'You don't think he's too young for me?'

'Mum, he's forty-seven, barely four years younger than you, hardly a toy boy!'

He certainly didn't look like one. Not that he was gross or anything but he was a bit overweight and, with his hair already receding, he looked older than Mum. But then that was no surprise 'cos Mum looked great for her age. With no artificial help either – well, apart from a splash of hair dye and the odd dab of anti-aging cream.

'Well, what then?' Mum said.

'What do you mean, what?'

Poor Mum looked confused, as if she was having trouble untangling the question.

'You just don't seem very keen,' Mum said at last.

'Well, it's not me that's marrying him, is it? So it doesn't matter.'

'It does matter, Jessie,' Mum said. 'I care about what you think.'

'I told you, I'm fine with it,' said Jessica, almost managing to convince herself. 'Jonathon's OK, I wouldn't mind him as a step-dad.'

Step-dad sounded well weird but hey, Jonathon was easy-going enough, not really the sort to interfere and it would only be for a couple of years anyway. After that she'd probably be off to university, like her brothers. So it wouldn't make much difference to her but she wasn't sure it was right for Mum.

'It's just that . . .' Jessica began. 'I mean do you love him?'

Jessica almost shuddered as she said it. It seemed wrong somehow, talking to Mum about love and stuff.

'Er, yes, of course I do.'

'Really love him, like you used to love Dad?'

Mum turned her head away, the slight movement giving Jessica her answer. She'd watched Mum and Jonathon together often enough and, OK, they got on – they liked the same sort of boring music and films, they even had a laugh together sometimes but something was missing – it wasn't like Mum had been with Dad.

Jessica glanced up at the digi-frame on her bookshelf, with its ever-changing display of photos. It had just switched from a fantastic one of her and Kal to another one of her favourites. There she was with Granddad, Mum, Dad and the boys on their eleventh birthday, when she was just seven. Life seemed so uncomplicated then, so normal, back in the days just before Granddad died. But even that hadn't been the root of it. Sure Dad had been a mess. He'd really struggled to cope with the shock, the way it had happened, but they'd got through it eventually, him and Mum together.

She couldn't remember in detail. She'd been so young and they hadn't told her everything at the time so it was all a bit patchy. She knew Dad had been off work for several months after Granddad's funeral. But no one had used the term 'breakdown' back then. No that must have come later when she got older and tried to piece things together. Maybe she didn't know everything, even now. Her parents had never been exactly keen to talk about it – totally ignored her questions most of the time so she'd stopped asking. But the point was that they'd got through it. Dad had gone back to teaching. Life had got back to normal. Or it seemed to.

'You've gone quiet, Jess,' Mum said. 'What are you thinking?'

'Nothing.'

But she was. She was thinking about how suddenly, five years ago, everything had changed again, big style. Mum and Dad had split just like that with no reason that anyone could see. There didn't seem to be anyone else involved at the time and Dad was still on his own, as far as she knew. She'd thought and thought about it but she was still no nearer working it out. At first she'd thought Dad had suffered another breakdown, some sort of relapse. There were no obvious signs so she was probably wrong. But there just didn't seem to be any other explanation.

'You were always so happy with Dad,' she said, eventually. 'I still don't understand . . .'

'No you don't, Jessie,' Mum snapped, 'and you probably never will. You only ever saw what was on the surface.'

Yeah right but most of the time the surface had looked pretty good to her. And it was the speed that really freaked her. It had all happened so quickly. One minute her parents had been fine and the next there'd been this chill between them, spreading through the family as if an ice age had settled on the house. Within a month or so, Dad had left the house, left his job at the school, which he'd always loved, and gone to teach English abroad. That was it, marriage, family life over, finished. Neither she nor Mum had seen or heard from him since, as far as she knew.

Sure Ben and Alex still kept in touch. They saw him whenever he was back in England, which wasn't very often these days with flight restrictions getting ever tighter. But her brothers could never tell her much.

'Dad seems OK,' they'd say. 'He asked about you, sends his love.'

Big, bloody deal! And, no, they'd say when she pushed them, he never talked about what happened, never explained why he was allowed to see them but not her and never explained why he didn't try harder to get access. Like it just didn't bloody matter! No, she knew that wasn't fair. Dad loved her, he did. She knew he'd want to see her, which is why it was so flaming hard to figure out what was stopping him. Well, not that hard actually – it was Mum who was stopping him.

She stared at Mum, wondering whether to push it further. Trouble was, if she asked, if she pushed it too much, if she said she wanted to see him, Mum just got angry, tearful, hysterical almost, not really like Mum at all. So Jessica'd sort of accepted it, learnt to leave it alone, just as she'd learnt not to talk about her granddad. But she hadn't given up, no way. In a year or two, when she was a bit older, she'd go and find Dad, find some answers. Mum couldn't stop her then. Mum wouldn't even need to know.

'Look, I'm sorry,' Mum said as if unnerved by the stare, 'it's late and I should never have started this. I should have waited till tomorrow. I just thought you'd be pleased for me.'

'I am pleased, Mum,' Jessica forced herself to say. 'If it's what you want.'

'It is,' said Mum, getting up, walking towards the door. 'Yes it is.'

Jessica turned off the light as soon as Mum left and lay on her back, wondering whether to phone Kal and tell him the news. She decided against it, on the grounds that it might not even happen. But if it did? What would Ben and Alex think when Mum told them? They hadn't even met Jonathon yet 'cos they didn't bother coming home much. Last Christmas they'd taken on a bar job at uni.

'Extra money and it cuts down on travel costs,' they said.

But it wasn't just that. They were happier away from home because home wasn't the same any more. God, she missed them – even though last time they came back they'd spent most of their time playing stupid, macho video games together! They didn't consciously shut her out though. It wasn't because she was adopted or anything nasty like that. Nothing to develop a complex about!

It was just – well, it was just the way it was. They were older, they were boys, they were twins, they had each other so they'd never really needed her. One thing was for sure, whatever they thought about Mum getting married again, they'd both think exactly the same way about it; they always did.

She kept her mind fixed on Alex and Ben for a while. It was easier to guess how the boys might react, than trying to untangle her own thoughts. She knew what she felt, what she'd always hoped. That was easy enough. She'd hoped Mum and Dad would get back together. Even after the divorce had come through, she'd gone on hoping. But that was fantasy land. She knew deep down it wasn't ever going to happen so there was no point making a fuss and spoiling things for Mum now.

If Mum thought she could be happy with Jonathon, fine, no probs. Satisfied with her own advice, she closed her eyes and did her deep breathing, counting herself to sleep, filing every-thing away back into their compartments: One, Dad, Two, Mum, Three, Jonathon, Four . . .

Cate wiped the condensation from the car window and peered out at the garage forecourt. She blinked. Shit, the sun was right in her eyes. It was so bloody early the sun had no right to be up but there it was beaming down at her all bright and happy. She blinked again. What was Iain doing, the idiot! He'd dropped the bloody petrol card. He was going to draw attention to himself, scrabbling about like that. Cate got out of the car and stretched, risking a quick sniff at her armpits at the same time.

They'd slept in the car again last night. They'd been so knackered they'd just stopped in a lay-by and crashed so she really, really needed to find somewhere to shower soon. Iain gave her a nervous sort of smile. He'd picked up the card but was still standing back from the petrol pump, as if the nozzle was suddenly about to leap out and club him over the head. She half wished it would, it might shake him up a bit!

'Cate, are you sure this will work?' he asked, holding the card between his finger and thumb.

'You won't know till you try, will you? Now hurry up.'

'But we could get arrested,' he whined. 'I've still got a few litres left on my card. Why don't we use that up and . . .'

'We're gonna have to use the fakes eventually,' she hissed. 'It'll be fine. Just do it!'

God he was such a wimp, such a jerk! But then again he was twenty-one, which impressed her mates, 'specially as he looked even older. His main attraction though was his driving licence. Not only that but he lived with a mega rich aunt and uncle who let him borrow a car and who didn't much care what he got up to. He probably got his money from them too 'cos he always seemed to have plenty. He was the richest student she knew – just what she needed. And it had taken bloody ages to find someone even half suitable so she absolutely couldn't risk a bust-up with him now. Not that it would come to that. Iain was hooked. He might moan and whine but, in the end, he'd do whatever she asked. Lads always did.

'Just swipe the bloody card, Iain. The woman in the kiosk's looking!'

'Card accepted,' the petrol pump said in the neutral monotone of most pre-programmed machines.

'See!' Cate said, as Iain quickly grabbed the pump as though he was expecting it to change its mind. 'You can buy anything on line if you've got enough money and you know where to look.'

She had to admit they made a good team. He had the money and there was nothing, but nothing, she couldn't do given any kind of computer and half an hour to spare. Fake petrol cards, easy-peasy, she had another five safely tucked away in her purse, each one with a full month's petrol ration. Hopefully they wouldn't need anything like that much, 'specially as the car was part electric, but however long it took, however many laws she had to break, she was going to find some answers.

She got back in the car and rewarded Iain with a quick kiss when he slid back into the driver's seat. Mmm – not too much of an ordeal. He was almost fanciable since she'd insisted he got his hair styled and bought some decent clothes. She let her fingers linger on the nape of his neck for a moment then pulled them away. No, she wasn't going to let the relationship get too deep or too physical and, mercifully, he wasn't pushy. Funny really, he was a bit odd like that; not like most of the lads she knew. He was so dull, bless him!

'So what now?' he asked.

She looked at the clock on the dashboard. It was only ten to nine so plenty of time.

'Now we find somewhere where I can have a wash or better still a shower. Then we have breakfast, then we go and check out the house again.'

'This is crazy, you know that, don't you?' he said, starting the engine. 'Which way?'

'Left, there's a hotel up the road, near that roundabout. I noticed it yesterday. They're bound to have decent washrooms.'

'Do you want to put the radio on,' he said, 'catch the news?'

'OK but there won't be anything. I told you. No one's looking for me and no one's reported me missing, all right?'

'I don't know how you can be so sure,' he said. 'It's Thursday, we've been gone since Sunday. Won't your – er – your . . .'

43

'Parents?' said Cate. 'Is that the word you're looking for?'

'Yeah,' said Iain, a faint blush creeping up his neck, 'they'll be really worried about you by now.'

'Well, they won't be very happy, that's for sure. But I left them a note. And they know I can look after myself and that I'll be back eventually. I've even sent a couple of texts so they won't go to the cops or anything.'

'They might. I mean, have you told them what you're doing, yet?'

'No! Now stop fretting and stop asking bloody questions. Even if they go to the cops, they won't do anything. I mean loads of girls take off with their boyfriends. It's not like I'm under age or anything. There's the hotel, look, just up ahead. Now remember, when we go in, don't skulk. The trick is to look like you're supposed to be there. We'll go in separately, OK? I'll go first. Give me a few minutes then you go in.'

That way if he got himself thrown out, it was his business. She'd have already found a washroom. It was even easier than she'd thought. She walked straight past the brain-dead bimbo on reception, past the low coffee tables with their vases of fresh flowers, and into the Ladies. No one else was in there, no one to disturb her while she washed and cleaned her teeth. Bliss! She even managed to give her hair a quick wash. She slipped into a cubicle to get changed then out again to do her make-up. She was just doing her mascara when the door opened and a middle-aged woman came in.

Cate stopped, half-turned and smiled. The woman smiled back as Cate knew she would. As the woman disappeared into a cubicle, Cate gave a last flick with the mascara and took a last look at her reflection. Her style was unusual, individual, granted, but she looked sooo good. She always did. She wasn't being vain. It was just the way she was. Clever, good-looking, popular, no problems – or at least that's what she'd thought until about eight months ago. Sure her upbringing had been a touch unconventional, in more ways than one, but it wasn't what you could call a problem. It had never bothered her. And if it bothered other people, well tough, that was their business. It had freaked Iain, it still did.

'You mean you've never ever been to school?' he'd almost shrieked, that day in the café, when she'd told him she was home educated and that these days she more or less taught herself.

He still went on about how she ought to go to college – like qualifications, bits of paper, actually mattered a toss, but he wasn't stupid enough to say anything about the stuff that really freaked him. She left the Ladies and walked out past reception, where Brain-Dead Bimbo was reading a magazine. Iain was already back in the car – if he'd ever plucked up the courage to go into the hotel at all.

'Look, I've been thinking,' he said as she got in.

'Well don't, let me do the thinking.'

'There must be a better way.'

'Maybe there is but this is good enough for me.'

'It's probably not what you think, anyway,' Iain whined. 'It's maybe just a coincidence.'

'Yeah, right!'

'Can't we just go home and talk to your parents? Even if they haven't been to the police or caused a fuss, they'll be dead worried about you, I know they will. And all this spying stuff is crazy, I mean, you don't even know . . .'

Cate sighed loudly, interrupting him. She knew a whole lot more than he thought. She hadn't told Iain everything, in fact she hadn't told him much at all yet. It was safer that way. Don't trust anybody!

'No, I don't,' she said. 'I don't know anything for sure. That's why I'm going to find out. Now just shut up and drive.'

3

Jessica closed her book, threw it down on the bed and switched on her laptop. That was the trouble with being an efficient sort of sleeper – you could never have a decent lie-in. She always woke up early, full of energy even on a day off after four days of hard labour at the supermarket followed by a late night. It had been barely six when she'd woken and she'd been out of bed by half past. It was nearly ten now and still Mum wasn't up, which was unusual even for a Thursday when Mum worked from home. But she wouldn't wake her just yet.

She picked up her phone and called Kaleem.

'Hey!' he drawled, sounding sleepy.

'You still in bed?'

'No chance! My stupid cousins woke me up ages ago throwing flaming pillows around but I've just dozed off again in a chair. Pity you woke me up 'cos I was having this like really amazing dream about you!'

'Nothing rude, I hope,' said Jessica, in the mock stern voice she usually reserved for Mum.

'Not telling,' said Kal, 'unless you tell me what you dreamt about first.'

'I never remember,' said Jessica, 'except for music. Does that count? I must hear music in my sleep 'cos I wake up with like all these tunes floating round my head. It was something sort of bouncy and classical this morning, so God knows what that was the soundtrack to!'

'You're weird, you know that!' Kal said. 'I guess that's why I love you.'

Jessica almost dropped the phone. The L word, he'd actually said the L word. He didn't mean it, not after only six weeks, he couldn't but hey, it sounded good!

'Oh, no,' he muttered, 'I'm gonna have to go. Mum's shouting me. We're supposed to be going shopping. More wedding stuff! Call you later. 'Bye.'

Jessica shuddered at the word wedding, which now only meant one thing. Mum and Jonathon. She looked at the time again wondering whether Mum was ever going to get up. Oh well, at least she'd had time to tidy her room up a bit and finish her book. Sol had survived – naturally – which was more than could be said for his poor girlfriend. The mad scientist had escaped so there'd surely be a sequel. Maybe it was already out. She could look it up, download it or even better, order a paper copy. Paper versions meant she'd have to wait a day or two but it was worth it, real books were way better. She ordered five books in the end then checked her messages. Mainly rubbish apart from one signed A&B.

Alex and Ben always did that. Messages and texts were always from both of them so you could never tell who'd actually written it. If Kaleem thought she was weird, what would he make of her brothers! Or maybe they weren't so odd; maybe all twins did stuff like that. She couldn't be sure. She didn't know any other twins apart from her brothers and they'd always acted totally in sync as if they were one person not two.

Their message was just chat, no mention of Dad, but at least they bothered – managed to remember they had a sister sometimes. She replied even though she didn't have much to say.

Hols dull so far, Kal away, work boring.

There was Mum's news from last night but she should let Mum tell them about that – if Mum decided to go ahead. With any luck she'd have second thoughts this morning, when the effect of the wine wore off. Anyway, best not to mention anything to Ben and Alex – not yet. She flicked instead to her web pages. She'd been meaning to update them for ages but hadn't got round to it.

'Oh, heck,' she groaned, 'worse than I thought!'

Her musical clips made her sound like an eight-year-old! Uh, even the colours were giving off the wrong messages – too cute, not her at all. It must have been mega ages since she updated.

'Gross!' she muttered, scowling at her pictures.

She'd had her hair cut and highlighted again since then. It had been Mum's post-exam treat – a girly day out to the beauty salon! OK, so some new pictures were needed, definitely.

'I hope you're careful what you put on there,' she could almost hear Mum saying.

Well she was; she was always careful. No giving away personal stuff or anything that could lead total strangers to her bank account – not that they'd find much in it! She'd only been working for a week or two, part-time Sundays to Wednesdays, and hadn't managed to save any of it. But she would – she'd set herself a target for the end of the hols. She flipped through her pages again. Most of what she'd posted was chat, trivia, rubbish. That 'true-life' ghost story, for a start.

'That can go,' she announced to the empty room.

She'd written it last October, around Halloween, when all her friends had been going on about ghosts and stuff, posting allegedly spooky pictures and stories. But hers just made her sound like a complete loon, totally childish! She didn't believe in ghosts or anything paranormal, which is why horror stories never scared her too much, but it had been dead freaky at the time – the only really weird thing that had ever happened to her. She jumped slightly as her bedroom door was suddenly flung open.

'It's gone ten o'clock,' Mum announced, standing there in her pale blue silky nightdress with her red-brown hair all ruffled. 'Why didn't you wake me?'

'I thought you'd want to lie in. You're working from home today, aren't you?'

'Yes but I've got tons to do. I should have started over an hour ago.'

'Quit panicking,' Jessica said. 'Go and have a shower. I'll get your computer set up and make you some breakfast, OK?'

'Thanks love, you're a star! I don't know what I'd do without you,' Mum said, darting off.

Mum appeared in the kitchen, ten minutes later just as Jessica was buttering the toast. No one could get ready quite as quickly as Mum and still manage to look moderately human! Jessica handed her a mug of coffee and the toast, which she started nibbling straight away. She didn't mention Jonathon or last night so maybe she was still mulling it over. Best not to pry, Mum would tell her in her own time.

'I had a message from the boys this morning,' Jessica said, as much to break the silence as anything.

'Are they OK?'

'Yeah, they seem to be. They're doing a bit of evening bar work as well as their day jobs, confusing all the customers, as usual. It must be dead weird being a twin.'

'Er, yes,' said Mum, between sips of coffee. 'I suppose it is.'

'Hey, do you remember that time at the museum when I thought I saw . . .'

'The museum?' said Mum, putting down the mug, sending coffee slopping everywhere. 'Yes, I remember, of course I remember, but that was ages ago. What's got you thinking about that silly business again? Was it that daft book you were reading?

You really ought to read something decent instead of filling your head with rubbish.'

'Mum!' said Jessica, grabbing a cloth and wiping up the coffee.

It wasn't like she only read pulp fiction. She read loads of different stuff, all kinds of books. Serious science books for a start but even that was wrong, according to Mum. She just couldn't win! Mum didn't want her to do science, she wanted her to do some boring business course, like the boys, or do English at university like both her and Dad had done but tough. She'd signed up for maths and science A levels and that was exactly what she was going to do.

'It was nothing to do with the book, OK?' Jessica said. 'I was thinking about Ben and Alex, that's all. Then earlier when I was updating my sites I came across . . .'

'What?' said Mum, glancing up at the kitchen clock.

'Nothing, look, it's nothing, just forget it. Has Jonathon been in touch?'

'Not since last night, no. I said I might meet him for lunch today.'

'And what are you going to tell him?'

'I won't be telling him anything, at this rate. I

won't have time to stop for lunch,' Mum said, getting up, the last piece of toast in her hand. 'I really need to get on.'

Jessica went back upstairs, back to her laptop. That's why Sol and people in stories didn't tell their parents stuff. They were always too busy, they didn't listen and when they did, they'd just tell you that you were 'silly'. OK, in this case it was probably dead right but that wasn't the point! She looked at her 'true-life' ghost story again. It seemed totally daft now, like Mum said, but it had definitely spooked her at the time.

It was our last school trip from juniors, she'd written, *the end of year treat! We got the train to London and headed to the Science Museum.*

She'd really been looking forward to it, she remembered. Even back in juniors, science had been her thing.

Trouble was every school in the country seemed to have had the same idea. It was so crowded!

Oh God, that rush of panic when she'd thought she'd lost her group. Turning round and round until she was almost dizzy, looking for flashes of dark blue jumpers. Then just as she'd spotted her class, seeing something else, someone else, someone who looked just like her. Their eyes meeting, for a nano-second, until they'd both turned away and she'd fled back to her pack.

That's all it had been; a glimpse, a freaky moment. She hadn't told her friends or her teachers at the time but she'd barely taken in any of the other exhibits, hadn't tried any of the interactives 'cos she'd been so busy looking for the girl in the maroon blazer; the girl who looked so much like her, as much as Ben and Alex were alike.

But I never found her, she read, her eyes drifting over the end of her story. *There were no school groups wearing maroon, or at least I didn't see any. And the girl did look very odd, very old-fashioned, more twentieth century than twenty-first, so was she a ghost?*

Certainly by the time she'd got home she'd totally convinced herself that what she'd seen was a ghost. As you do when you're barely eleven!

'It was a mirror, you dozo,' Ben, or was it Alex, had said.

'But she was wearing different clothes.'

'Duh! Science museum, virtual reality, you press a button to see yourself as a Roman Centurion or early twentieth-century schoolgirl.'

'No, it wasn't like that. I hadn't pressed any buttons.'

'Well, it's no big deal,' Dad had claimed, 'lots of people look similar.'

'Doppelgänger,' one of the twins had added, 'a double, loads of people have them. Think of all the celebrity look-alikes. I read somewhere that everyone has at least one double. I mean, we share about seventy per cent of our genes with an earth worm, right, not to mention about forty per cent with a dandelion. So imagine how many you share with another person.'

The stats the twins had thrown at her might not have been right or she might not have remembered them properly but it was near enough. She'd read something very similar recently – maybe at school 'cos she remembered Kal saying it was pretty weird to think you were almost half dandelion!

'You were scared, you said you'd got dizzy, you imagined it that's all. It wasn't a double and it certainly wasn't a ghost,' Dad had said, when she'd gone on and on about it.

'And I couldn't have a twin, could I?' she'd asked, looking at the boys. 'I mean, when I was adopted, was there . . .'

She'd known it was a daft idea but she'd been looking for logical explanations, something to steer her away from ghosts!

'No,' Mum had said, 'there was only you and you've imagined the similarity, now stop being silly.'

Maybe Mum had been right. Maybe the whole thing was imagination, something she'd conjured up – some sort of bad omen – because soon after that Dad had left and the family fell apart. Jessica looked at her laptop again, moved a few pictures around and deleted her story. She'd hyped-up a fair bit anyway, making it seem far spookier than it really was. That was the idea, it was a Halloween story, but it wasn't a ghost she'd seen, not least because there was no such thing!

It hadn't been an omen either and it really didn't mean anything. It was nothing, absolutely nothing. With the story deleted, the page looked a complete mess now but tough, she'd sort the rest later, if she could be bothered. She'd arranged to meet all her friends in town at twelve. OK so Kal wouldn't be there but it was the first big get-together of the holidays and she didn't want to be late.

Louise jogged along the park path, listening to her music, the light rain blowing in her face, her hair flopping in her eyes. She stopped, pushed the hair back behind her ears and looked round. The park was empty but she had a funny feeling that

she wasn't alone, that someone was watching her.
Shivering slightly she hurried on, looking right, left,
then glancing behind.

As she turned back, a youngish man stepped out
from behind a tree, right in front of her, blocking
her path. He was wearing a black top, blue jeans
and a black cap pulled down so she couldn't see
his eyes, just the long nose and sneering mouth.
But it wasn't his clothes or his face that her eyes
fixed on. It was the knife, the glinting knife in his
right hand; the blade already flashing towards her
as she started to scream.

Screaming on and on, thrashing around until she
felt the softness of the pillows and the tangle of
the duvet. The screams turned to sobs but there
was no one to hear. Louise sat up, forcing away
the dream and the tears, making herself remember
who she was, where she was, when she was.

OK, OK, it was Thursday, the day after her
appointment. She hadn't slept well, no surprise
there, but she'd got up early, been for her swim
and by the time she got back her parents had
already gone off to see Great-Aunt Mary, as they
did every Thursday. She'd been shattered so she'd
flopped on her bed. How long had she slept? She

glanced at the clock. Quarter past eleven so not long but long enough to have slipped into the nightmare, the same bloody nightmare she always had.

There were variations, sometimes it was clear, like it was really happening, sometimes it was more hazy and sometimes it went on longer. Those were the worst dreams, when she was somehow hovering above the path, looking down on herself, at the multiple stab wounds, ripped clothes, blood everywhere. But, whatever the variations, the park, the route, the soft classical music and the man with the knife were always the same. And no matter how many times she had the dream, even when it was hazy, it always seemed totally real almost like every time was the first time.

Where did it come from, why did she have the same flaming nightmare over and over? Was it some film she'd seen once? She'd been about six or seven when the nightmares first started. It was around the time they'd moved to Harrogate, so maybe it was some sort of fear thing; fear of the unknown. Or perhaps it was a premonition, something that would really happen one day. Because the Louise in the dream had always been grown-up, older even than she was now, so maybe this was something that was going to happen in the future.

Not very likely, she had to admit. Certainly not the way it happened in the dream. She never went jogging for a start; jogging wasn't really her thing and she was pretty sure that the park wasn't one she'd ever seen for real. So nothing whatsoever to do with real life and probably not an omen, a warning; more likely it was just a stress dream. Now stress really was her thing, she was well good at stressing! She could stress for Britain as Daddy always said. Maybe she should tell someone, get a dream analyst onto it or something. It might go away if she shared it with someone but then again they'd probably just tell her she was mad!

She swung her legs over the side of the bed, her feet touching something soft and furry. She looked down to see one of the cats curled up, apparently not bothered about being trodden on. She bent down, stroking Tip's sleek, black fur. Pets were supposed to be calming. It helped a bit but not quite enough to shake off the nightmare so she slipped her shoes on, the new ones, and stood up.

No point sitting around thinking about it, making herself feel sick but what to do? Her parents wouldn't be back for ages and she didn't fancy hanging round the house on her own. She could walk round to Gina's, talk her into going into town and maybe do some shopping. Shopping was good, a bit of retail therapy always cheered her up.

She looked out of the bedroom window onto the massive back garden where two of her other cats, the youngest ones, were chasing each other round, up and down the trees. It was slightly over-cast, not quite as hot as yesterday but at least it didn't look like rain so she wouldn't need a jacket. She picked up her bag and headed downstairs but with each step her stomach churned a bit more and by the time she reached the front door her legs were shaking.

Maybe she could call Gina and ask her to come round or she could just stay home and shop on line. No, it was stupid. It was barely a ten-minute walk, she didn't have to go through any parks and the only trees she had to pass were the ones at the bottom of her own front driveway. She couldn't let the nightmare get to her, she couldn't give in to a stupid dream and fears about people following her or she'd end up like Great-Aunt Mary, suspicious, paranoid and totally agoraphobic.

Aunt Mary never went out any more, never went beyond her own front gate, which is why her parents had to go round two or three times a week to make sure her deliveries had arrived, that she had everything she needed, that she hadn't barricaded herself into her bedroom again. How long could they go on like that, how long would it be before Mary had to go into a home? That's what happened when you couldn't cope. You got shoved in some institution. And she didn't fancy a psychiatric unit, no way!

Forcing herself to take a deep breath she checked that she'd got her key-card and stepped outside. She closed the door firmly and set off down the long drive. Walking down the drive was never a problem, apart from when it was icy, but walking back up the slope could be a bit of a pain with heavy school bags or bags of shopping. Maybe her new strappy shoes with heels were a mistake if she was going to be tramping round shops for the rest of the day.

She paused at the bend of the drive, near the apple trees, looking down at her shoes, wondering whether she should go back and change into her trainers. She looked back towards the house. No she couldn't be bothered, she'd manage. If she went back to the house she might start fretting again. She turned to set off down the rest of the drive but froze as she caught a hint of movement behind the trees. It might be the cats but none of them usually came down here, they tended to go through the cat-flap out the back.

'Who is it?' she said. 'Who's there?'

OK, it was cats or her imagination or a bird hopping about or something, but she wasn't taking any chances. She started to edge back but she'd only managed a short step when her legs started shaking and she saw him, stepping out right in front of her. She couldn't move, couldn't speak, couldn't breathe. Her head was starting to spin, her eyes barely functioning as she tried to take in the blur of blue jeans, dark top. No, this wasn't happening, it couldn't be right. She was awake, she wasn't dreaming. It was OK. It wasn't the same as the dream. He was younger; there was no park, no jogging, no music, no cap and no knife.

There was no knife, she was safe – it wasn't the same. But who was he, why was he here, what was he doing? He moved away from her slightly, like he was scared, his hand slipping into his pocket. Oh God, he was pulling something out. This was it, he had a knife! She was going to die. She saw a glint of silver, heard rapid footsteps, saw someone else hurrying up the drive towards them.

The lad glanced behind, still clutching the silvery thing – a phone, an old-fashioned mobile, not a knife. The other person had almost reached them, sending Louise's brain into overdrive, making her heart race. This was definitely it. She'd finally flipped, this other person just couldn't be real; the hallucinations had kicked in.

Louise felt her legs weakening, her body crumpling as she tried to scream.

4

The door of the café tinkled as Dr Jay pushed it open and, before she'd taken more than a step inside, Carla was there, wiping her hands on the front of her green and white striped overall, although clearly her hands weren't dirty.

'You took your time,' Carla hissed, looking around at the crowded tables. 'It's almost lunchtime, we're busy.'

'I came as soon as I could.'

'You call this soon! I've been asking you since Monday.'

Dr Jay sighed. She'd initially told them she'd be there by the end of the week but that wasn't good enough. Their messages had got more frequent, more paranoid, until the one that interrupted her session with Louise yesterday had prompted her to change her plans.

'I was busy,' she explained. 'I had things to do,

people to see, things to clear up first. Anyway I don't know why you needed to see me in person.'

'It's not me as much as Tess, she's in a right state,' Carla said, ushering Dr Jay through to the back, muttering instructions to her staff at the same time.

The kitchen was hot, steamy, with staff bustling round, all in the same green and white overalls with net hats, so it took a moment to pick out Tess crouching by one of the ovens.

'I could come back a bit later,' said Dr Jay. 'An hour or two won't make any difference. I can have a walk round. I haven't been to Edinburgh for years.'

'No,' said Tess, standing up, quickly whipping off her oven gloves, as if she feared Dr Jay would simply disappear. 'No, the staff can cope for a while. We'll talk now.'

Tess led the way outside to a tiny courtyard, full of large bins, sickly smells and a few sad plants wilting in pots. She pulled off the rather unflattering, flimsy kitchen hat she'd been wearing and shook her short, blonde hair into place. Her narrow face, usually quite pale, was still flushed from the heat of the ovens.

'So when was the last time you heard from Cate?' Dr Jay asked.

'Early this morning,' said Tess. 'She sent another message saying she was safe, she was fine. She said she just fancied a few days away.'

'But you don't believe her?'

Tess raised her neatly plucked eyebrows by way of an answer.

'And this boy she's with, this Iain?' Dr Jay said.

'He's all right,' said Carla, glancing at Tess. 'Cate's only been going out with him a couple of months but we've known him longer. He's a student but he's living with some relatives. He comes to the café. He's a nice lad – mature, sensible.'

'He's a fair bit older than Cate,' said Tess, 'but a lot less worrying than her usual choice of boyfriends.'

Looks were passing between Tess and Carla all the time, anxious and furtive, like they were hiding something but then wasn't everybody?

'So you don't think she's in any danger?' Dr Jay asked.

'No,' said Tess, 'but that's not the point.'

'So what is?'

'I thought you could tell me,' said Tess, starting to pace the empty middle section of the tiny court-yard. 'Has she been in touch?'

'No,' said Dr Jay, 'she couldn't, unless you gave her my number.'

'I didn't,' said Tess, 'but that wouldn't stop her! You know Cate! She's so bloody smart, so tenacious. She knows something. She knows we've lied to her.'

'Did she tell you that?'

More furtive looks passing between Tess and Carla.

'No,' said Tess, 'not as such.'

'She started asking a lot of questions again,' said Carla, 'earlier this year. Just after New Year in fact.'

'And we told her what we'd always told her,' said Tess, 'but I could see she didn't believe it any more. I could see it in her eyes, the way she looked at me.'

'Why didn't you tell me at the time?' Dr Jay snapped. 'Why didn't you tell me about the questions?'

'Carla didn't think it was anything,' said Tess. 'And anyway the questions stopped for a while but Cate changed. She didn't talk to us so much. She started spending more time in her room.'

'She's a teenager!' said Dr Jay. 'It's what they do!'

It seemed that they'd dragged her all this way for nothing. It was all a false alarm and they were overreacting, as she'd first thought.

'You weren't here,' said Tess, 'you didn't see! She doesn't trust us any more, she doesn't believe us.'

'So why should she suddenly have stopped believing you? What could she have found out?'

'We thought you could tell us!' Tess snapped.

'She's even started asking for DNA tests recently,' Carla added before Dr Jay could respond to Tess or figure out any possible hidden meanings behind the words.

'And what did you say?' Dr Jay asked.

'I said we'd get one done, at her next appointment with you,' Tess said.

'You want me to fake the results?'

'Can you do that?' said Tess. 'Oh, I don't know, even if you can I don't think it's going to matter. She's definitely onto something, I know she is.'

Dr Jay fixed her eyes on one of the wilting potted plants. All right – so it was looking more likely that this was no false alarm. It was possible Cate was onto something. More possible than Tess or Carla could even begin to imagine but what to do about it, that was the thing.

'This is your fault!' Tess was saying. 'I don't see

why we had to lie to her. Why didn't you let us tell her the truth?'

'The truth!' said Dr Jay. 'And how do you think she'd have coped with that?'

'She'd have been all right,' said Tess, 'if we'd told her bit by bit as she was growing up, letting her get used to it . . .'

Her voice got quieter as she spoke, finally trailing off completely, giving way to tears. She took the tissue Carla offered and blew her nose.

'And if she'd told anybody, blurted it out, like children do,' Dr Jay asked, 'what do you think would have happened then?'

'I don't know,' Tess said between sobs. 'It's such a mess. We should never have done it, we should never have agreed to it. It was crazy, it was wrong.'

Dr Jay closed her eyes momentarily. Other people had said those words to her, more than once. But it wasn't true. She hadn't done anything wrong.

'You mean you wish you'd never had Cate?' said Dr Jay, opening her eyes, looking straight at Tess. 'You wish she'd never been born.'

Tess shook her head and leant against the wall.

'Cate means everything to me,' she said quietly. 'You know she does. I couldn't imagine life without Cate. But every time I look at her, I think of – oh

God, I don't know what I think – but if we lose her now!'

'You won't lose her,' said Dr Jay. 'I won't let that happen. I'll find her, I'll deal with it.'

'So how are you going to find her,' said Carla, 'unless we go to the police?'

She stressed the last word, with a hint of challenge in her voice.

'Maybe they'd be able to track her messages,' Carla added.

'No!' said Dr Jay. 'There's no need for that. If she's really onto something, I think I know where she might have gone.'

'What?' said Tess. 'How? Is there something you haven't told us?'

Oh yes, there was one crucial point she hadn't ever told them. She'd always known it would come out in the end. It was a miracle it had stayed secret for so long. There were so many ways it might have been discovered. She'd been lucky or very clever so far but it couldn't last indefinitely. There were too many people involved, too much information out there. Sooner or later one of them would start to question, to piece things together. Some of them, like Tess and Carla, knew part of it. Others already knew the whole story but they also knew it was in their best interest to keep quiet. Not Cate though, Cate wouldn't keep quiet. If Cate found out the truth, it was all over unless . . .

'Tell us,' Carla was saying. 'If you know where she's gone, if you know what's happening, if there's something we need to know, tell us.'

There it was again, that hint of challenge in Carla's voice. As if Carla and Tess were somehow testing her, as if they knew more than they were letting on. Or it could just be that they were stressed. Maybe she was reading too much into their reactions. Dr Jay checked the time. There were a couple of possibilities where Cate might have gone; one slightly more likely than the other. If she left now, if she got the fast train, she could be there by early evening. Not that she'd be exactly welcome, but it couldn't be helped.

'I will,' said Dr Jay. 'If I'm right, if I find her, I'll tell you. I promise.'

But she could tell by their faces that they didn't believe her.

Cate glared at Iain before glancing down at Louise who was lying on the path.

'Oh great,' she said, 'just bloody great. Look what you've done!'

'Me?' said Iain. 'It's not my fault.'

'Oh sure, I only popped back to the car for two minutes! I told you to stay out of sight. What the hell happened?'

'She heard me, she saw me. She was terrified, really terrified. She probably thought I was gonna mug her or something. Then she just fainted.'

'Couldn't you have just asked for directions, made out like you were lost?'

'Like she'd believe that! I mean, why would I have left my car out on the road and wandered up her drive?'

'I don't friggin' know but you could have made up some excuse!'

'There wasn't time, it all happened so fast. I didn't know what to do. It wasn't my fault. I told you we shouldn't have come here. Not like this, not without any warning.'

'Yeah, yeah,' said Cate, 'but she wasn't supposed to see us, was she? Not yet, anyway. Now quit the lecture and help me to get her up before she goes and dies on us.'

The conversation had been slowly filtering through to Louise's brain and the mention of dying hit her at the same time as she felt someone bending over her, touching her arms. There were two of them – the lad and the other one – the girl who'd been running up the path. No, there was no girl, no lad, this wasn't real, it wasn't happening. But she could feel them, they were holding onto her, trying to pull her up.

'Get off me, leave me alone,' she screamed, squirming on the ground, shaking them off, twisting her left wrist round, reaching out with her right hand trying to get to her com.

'If you want to call for help, use this,' said the girl, bending down, handing her a phone like the lad's only this one was black not silver. 'Those coms are useless. Don't know how they ever caught on. I made Iain get rid of his. Honestly, you'll get RSI fiddling with those things, not to mention a seriously arthritic wrist by the time you're thirty.'

Louise stared at the phone as if it was a huge, black poisonous spider. Was it a trick? What kind of attackers offered you their phone to call for help: imaginary ones, that's who! But they looked and sounded and felt so real. So this was what it was like for Great-Aunt Mary, not knowing the difference, never being sure.

'Bit retro, I know,' the girl was saying, 'but it's cheap, I like it and it works. Here take it. Call the cops if you must but I don't think you really want to.'

'Who are you?' said Louise, ignoring the phone, looking instead at the lad, who looked nothing like the man in the nightmare, then back at the girl who really, really, couldn't be real.

'Get up, stop being so pathetic and I'll tell you,' said the girl.

Louise somehow managed to scramble to her feet but her legs wouldn't support her properly, her stomach was churning and she had to lean against one of the trees.

'This is Iain,' said the girl, 'and I'm Cate.'

'It's all right, Katherine. Just relax.'

Dr Jay's words burst into Louise's head, ripping through the tangle of other crazy information that refused to gel, refused to give any sensible explanation for what was happening, the impossibility of what she was seeing. It was so totally, totally freaky.

'Kate, that's short for Katherine, right?' Louise managed to say, the words forcing themselves out in short, breathless bursts.

'Wrong,' said the girl. 'Cate, an amalgam of Carla and Tess.'

'What?'

'CA for Carla, TE for Tess,' the girl said slowly,

as if Louise was a total idiot. 'My mums are called Carla and Tess. They thought it was a sweet idea, at the time, to combine the names, yeah?'

'Er, your mums, plural?' said Louise, noticing that Iain was shaking his head, as if warning her to stop.

'Yes,' said Cate, drawing out the final 's' like a snake hissing, 'mums plural, as in two of them. Two mums, no dad. You *have* heard of civil partnerships, same sex marriages, in Harrogate, have you?'

'Er, yes, of course.'

'Oh good, that's absolutely super then,' said Cate, her soft Scottish accent replaced by a mocking version of Louise's voice. 'Iain's heard of them too but he still has trouble with it.'

'No I don't,' Iain muttered, 'I really like Tess and Carla, you know I do.'

'So,' said Louise, her eyes now fixed on the girl, taking in every centimetre of her face, her body, her clothes, seeing possible explanations, connections that made her stomach churn. 'So if they're . . . I mean you must be . . . er, I guess you were adopted.'

'Wrong again,' said Cate, 'my name's not Katherine and I'm not adopted.'

'Oh, so,' Louise began, wondering why she was even bothering to talk to these people her brain had conjured up.

'Look,' said Cate, nodding in the direction of the house, 'if we're going to compare family histories, as I really think we must, can we go inside?'

'Er, I don't think,' said Louise, 'I mean Mummy and Daddy . . .'

'Mummy and Daddy,' said Cate in the mocking voice again, 'are out, aren't they? So we'll be fine.'

Cate had started to walk towards the house. How did she know that, how did she know her parents were out?

'It was you, wasn't it?' Louise asked, hurrying to catch up with Cate, whilst Iain strode beside her. 'You've been watching me, haven't you – you've been following me and watching the house?'

'Very nice it is too,' said Cate, 'but don't worry, Lou, we're not after the family silver.'

'Cate don't,' said Iain, as Louise fumbled for her key-card, dropping it in the porch, as Cate said her name casually, like they were old friends or something. 'You're upsetting her.'

He picked up the key-card, smiling at Louise as he stood up. Cate glanced at the card then up at the cameras.

'All very high-tech and secure,' she said. 'Are the cameras on?'

'No,' said Louise, 'I don't think so. We only really use the security stuff at night.'

Why had she said that, why didn't she lie, make out that everything was being recorded? She reached out to try to take the card off Iain but he held on to it, shaking his head slightly as he looked at her trembling fingers.

'It's OK,' he said, his accent stronger but somehow more gentle than Cate's. 'It's all right. I know it's a shock.'

Shock! Shock didn't even begin to cover it. Her body, her head felt as if they were being squeezed in a giant clamp so she could barely draw breath, barely think. There were connections, possibilities but she couldn't focus, couldn't get past the whispering voice: *this isn't real, this isn't real.* But if it was real, was she doing the right thing letting them into the house? Could she stop them now, even if she wanted to? Maybe she should have taken her chance, phoned for help, but it was too late, Iain was already opening the door.

'Come on,' he said, 'it's OK, I promise. Where's the kitchen, I'll get you some water.'

Water, as if a glass of water was going to make

any difference but she took them to the kitchen anyway, flopped onto one of the chairs, put her head between her hands, rubbing at her eyes, willing her heart to keep beating, even if it was thumping far too fast.

'We're still here,' Cate said when Louise looked up again. 'We're real. It's not a dream.'

Louise squeaked as Cate pinched the top her arm, hard.

'Cate!' said Iain, who'd been opening cupboard doors, finding a glass. 'Just leave her alone, eh?'

'Only trying to help,' said Cate.

Cate shrugged, walked round the kitchen and sat at the other side of the table, directly opposite Louise, while Iain filled the glass. He brought it over and sat down next to Louise, pushing the glass towards her.

'Sip it, slowly,' he said, smiling at her again.

He had a nice smile, sort of shy but real, genuine. Louise stared at him as she took the first sip of her drink, taking in the details. The light brown hair, the even lighter eyebrows, the hazel-brown eyes, the small clump of freckles on the bridge of his nose, the tiny, tiny spot under the middle of his bottom lip, the narrow hands that were resting on the table; narrow hands, long slim fingers, spoilt a bit by the stubby chewed nails.

He was attractive though – but in an ordinary sort of way. There was something reassuring about him, he seemed sort of average, normal. It was certainly much easier looking at him than at the girl, easier to believe he was real, but she couldn't stare at him forever. She had to confront the freakiness that was Cate. She looked at Cate again, trying to control the explosions in her head.

'Who are you?' she asked.

'I thought we'd been through all this,' said Cate, suppressing a yawn, which might or might not have been real.

'But,' said Louise looking directly into the oh-so-familiar pale blue eyes, 'you look like – you look like me! You look exactly like me.'

'A bit slimmer and a bit more stylish, obviously,' said Cate, running her right hand through her short hair, flashed with multi-coloured highlights, 'but yeah, well spotted. I thought you'd never notice.'

5

'Louise, you can close your mouth now,' Cate said.

Louise didn't think her mouth was open, at least not very wide but she couldn't be sure because she didn't seem to have control of her limbs or mouth or anything else. She hadn't had a grip on anything from the moment she'd seen Cate. Her head had started to move slightly from side to side as if trying to shake her thoughts into place, trying to form some sort of sentence, some question to which there might just be a logical answer.

'You've had surgery, right,' she managed to say, 'to make yourself look like me?'

She knew it sounded crazy but she couldn't think of any other explanation.

'That's right,' said Cate, 'we thought we'd murder you then I can take your place, inherit all the money.'

Louise leapt up, or at least she tried to leap up

but her legs got tangled in the chair, so she fell over, pulling the chair on top of her.

'Oh for God's sake, Cate,' Iain said, picking up the chair, as Louise rubbed at her head then her ankle.

'Well, honestly,' said Cate, 'surgery, how mad is that?'

Iain stretched out his hand to Louise, helping her up.

'It's all right,' he said, while Cate laughed. 'She's joking. We're not going to hurt you, OK?'

Louise believed him. He didn't seem like a murderer somehow. But if the girl with the weird sense of humour hadn't had surgery, where did that leave them?

'So er,' Louise began, as she sat down again, glaring at Cate, 'I mean, what, how . . .'

The words she wanted to say wouldn't come out but Cate nodded, as if she understood.

'Now there's the thing,' said Cate, leaning towards her, 'why do we look so alike? Iain thinks it's a co-incidence, bless him, but I'm not so sure.'

'It must be,' said Louise, 'it has to be.'

'Does it?' said Cate, sharply.

'I don't know,' Louise admitted, grasping at a half-buried memory, the realization that she might have seen this girl before. 'I mean, how did you even know about me, how did you find me?'

'Let's skip the first bit for now,' said Cate, 'but finding you was easy. Have you any idea how much information you give away on-line?'

'No, I mean I don't, I'm sure I don't.'

'Well, put it this way,' said Cate, 'I could have found you ages ago but I thought I'd check out some information, get my facts straight first and believe me, there's not much I don't know about you.'

'Like what?'

'I know what school you go to, who your friends are, what you do in your spare time, your favourite film and the names of all your cats.'

'Well, yes,' said Louise, 'all that's on my web pages. It's not private.'

'No,' said Cate, 'and on the surface, we haven't got much in common, thank God, apart from our looks, of course.'

Cate looked at Iain, smiling like they were sharing a secret then looked around the kitchen as if she was assessing, mentally taking measurements and making comparisons.

'My house would just about fit into this kitchen, for a start,' said Cate, 'and we haven't exactly got similar tastes.'

'And you're older than me,' said Louise.

'Am I?' said Cate. 'What makes you think that?'

Louise looked at Cate's leggings, at the tight black top. She tried to look past the heavily made up eyes, the glossy lips, the long painted nails and the multi-coloured hair that managed to look spiky and softly ruffled at the same time. Cate looked about twenty.

'I'm sixteen,' said Cate, 'like you. Two months younger, allegedly, but who knows because if you dig a little deeper, Lou, you find some pretty freaky stuff.'

It was already way too freaky. Just sitting opposite this girl was freaky enough. Louise wasn't sure she wanted to delve any deeper but the words were already out.

'Like what?'

'Well, have you got any special powers, can you mind-read or make stuff move without touching it?'

'No,' said Louise, shifting in her chair, sitting up straight, 'wow, no, I don't think so. Can you?'

'No, you dozo,' said Cate, laughing, 'I'm just kidding!'

'Well, don't,' said Louise, putting her head down again to hide the growing redness of her cheeks. 'It's not funny, none of this is funny.'

'OK,' said Cate, 'no powers but I'm right about the freaky stuff.'

'How freaky?'

'You tell me,' said Cate, standing up, 'you've been to posh schools, you're supposed to be clever, work it out. Mind if I have a drink, you got any juice?'

Louise raised her head and nodded towards the fridge; while Cate found a glass she didn't say anything; she couldn't because she had no idea what Cate was on about.

'I'll give you a clue,' said Cate, pouring the orange juice. 'Parents.'

The word lodged in Louise's head, along with images of her own parents and hazy, imagined images of Cate's. She knew there had to be comparisons, connections somewhere but she couldn't quite work it out, not with Cate leaning against the work surface watching her like she was some particularly nasty specimen in a jar. There was something compelling, hypnotic almost about Cate. It was like looking in a mirror, sure, but a distorted mirror. Cate was so sharp, so confident; there was something dangerous about Cate.

'Well?' Cate asked.

'You said you weren't adopted,' Louise began. 'But your parents are . . .'

'Both female,' Cate said, 'and your parents are both old. Got it yet?'

'Well,' said Louise, slowly, 'my parents had fertility treatment.'

'I know.'

'How? How could you know that? I don't exactly share that kind of information on my web pages. I've never told anybody, I'm not allowed.'

'OK,' said Cate, 'so I didn't know for sure but I guessed. They're bloody pensioners for Christ's sake, not an enormous mental leap is it?'

'How do you know how old they are?'

'I checked out their company website,' said Cate, casually, as if prying into other people's business was second nature, which it probably was, 'and took it from there. Anyway, they had treatment, right?'

'And one of your mums,' said Louise, 'used a donor, I guess.'

'That's what they told me,' said Cate, putting down her glass and folding her arms. 'Such a sweet story. They whip an egg from Tess, fertilize it from an anonymous sperm donor, then – here comes the clever bit – pop it back into Carla so she gets to carry the baby and both mums feel involved. How good is that?'

'Can they do that?' said Louise.

'Oh sure they can,' said Cate, 'the wonders of modern medicine and all that. I'm not saying it's that common but it's possible and it happens.'

'So,' said Louise, sipping her water as the fireworks started in her head again, 'you're saying that my father might have been the donor, that when my parents were having the treatment . . .'

She paused. Could that be right, same father, different mother, could they end up looking so very similar?

'No,' said Cate. 'I'm saying it's all total bollocks.' She unfolded her arms and sat down again opposite Louise. 'I'm saying our parents lied to us.'

The word 'no' screamed in Louise's head but she didn't say it because what Cate said made sense, in a way. The way her parents had always been so cagey, so secretive about those check-ups for a start. Then there'd been times, many times, when Louise had felt wrong, out of place, as if she'd been born to the wrong people like when she tried to talk to them about music or art or books and they just didn't get it. Her parents really didn't have a creative or imaginative brain cell between them. Not to mention their ages – all the times she'd wanted younger parents, normal parents like her friends'.

But then loads of people felt that way. There was no such thing as normal parents, normal families. Nearly everyone she knew was embarrassed by their parents in one way or other. Poor Gina could barely look at her dad when he was with his new wife who was only twenty-six and Naomi's mum was a vicar who turned up at school to take assemblies sometimes. How embarrassing was that?

'Earth calling Louise!'

Cate's mocking voice broke into her thoughts.

'Sorry, I was thinking.'

'You ought to get together with Iain,' said Cate. 'Iain thinks, don't you, Iain? Not that it does him any good.'

Louise turned to look at Iain. He'd been so quiet, she'd almost forgotten he was there and, by the look on his face, he rather wished he wasn't. What was it with these two anyway, were they an item or just friends? He was clearly older than Cate and they seemed so different, somehow. Did it matter, why was she even thinking about it? There were way more important things to get her head around.

'And the result of all this thinking is?' Cate prompted.

'They wouldn't have lied to me,' said Louise, 'not about something like that.'

Even as she said it, she knew she wasn't sure.

'Why should they,' she pressed on, trying to convince herself, 'if there was no fertility treatment, if I was adopted or something, they could have said! Anyway, I couldn't have been. Mummy was definitely pregnant. What's funny now?'

'The way you say Mummy,' said Cate, 'like you were six not sixteen. Anyway, for what it's worth my *mummy* was definitely pregnant too.'

'OK,' said Louise, standing up, pushing her chair back.

Everything was moving so fast. There were things she needed to say, questions she needed to ask but Cate kept throwing information at her, mocking her, confusing her, as if it was possible to be more confused. She couldn't help feeling Cate was playing with her; that Cate knew a whole lot more than she was letting on.

'OK,' Louise said again, 'our parents could be telling the truth. What if they thought they were having treatment, what if that's what they were told? Only it wasn't their own eggs that were implanted back.'

'Ah, the Cuckoo Theory,' said Cate, 'eggs in other birds' nests and all that. Yeah, I've been down that route.'

'And?'

'It's possible,' said Cate, 'biological twins implanted in different wombs. Not bad, so go on, any other ideas?'

'Well,' said Louise, feeling her imagination kicking in, running wild, 'what if our parents' babies died at birth and they got us instead!'

'That's The Omen Theory,' Cate said.

'What?'

'*The Omen*, it's an old horror film. Couple's own baby's murdered and they get little Damon or Damien or whatever he's called, instead. Spawn of the devil, the Anti-Christ.'

Louise could almost believe that Cate was some sort of devil child but not her, no way.

'All right,' said Louise, 'if you know everything, if you've already worked it all out, why are you asking me?'

'Oh I haven't worked it all out,' said Cate, 'nowhere near. But I've run through a fair few ideas.'

'And don't you think they're all a bit far-fetched?' said Iain, turning slightly, appealing to Louise. 'I mean why would anyone do that, switch eggs, or switch babies?'

'I don't know,' said Louise, walking round to

the end of the table, ideas bursting through her head that were way more far-fetched than that, 'but I wouldn't put anything past Dr Jay.'

'Ah,' said Cate, 'I wondered when we'd get round to our mysterious doctor.'

'You know her?' said Louise.

'Oh yes,' said Cate, 'I know her and I sort of guessed you might but I didn't know for certain till yesterday.'

'It was you,' said Louise, 'in the blue car. You followed us all the way to Derby!'

'I've been checking you out for days,' said Cate. 'Hadn't a clue where you were off to yesterday but as soon as you turned off down that lane, I knew 'cos it's the sort of place she always picks.'

Always picks! So Cate had visits to Dr Jay in out of the way places too.

'It's all right, Katherine, just relax.'

'Are you sure your real name isn't Katherine?' Louise asked.

'Uh, yes! I might not know much about what's going on but I do know my own bloody name,' said Cate. 'Anyway, Iain didn't believe me about Dr Jay, of course, so we hung around just to make sure.'

'And about an hour after you left,' said Iain, 'a

van turned up, loaded a whole load of stuff and drove off.'

'But there's nothing weird going on, is there, Iain?' said Cate. 'It's all a coincidence. Our parents get treatment from the same doctor and end up with identical babies who Dr Jay monitors year after year – all perfectly normal!'

OK, so if Dr Jay saw Cate too then it definitely wasn't about kids born to older parents. It probably wasn't about babies who were slightly premature or any of the other stuff her parents had told her either. It was about babies, girls, who looked exactly the same! But had her parents lied or had Dr Jay lied to them?

'So who is she,' said Louise, 'what do you know about her?'

'What time are your parents due back?' said Cate, ignoring Louise's questions.

'In an hour or so, I guess. Oh God, what am I going to tell them, what am I going say? If they see you they'll totally freak.'

There was a sudden crash as the cat flap opened. Lucky and Lulu dived in and started chasing each other round the kitchen.

'Lively, aren't they!' said Cate.

'They're still only kittens really,' said Louise.

'Their mum's upstairs. She's a rescue cat. I found her injured on the road. Mummy wasn't keen on keeping Tip, especially when we realized she was pregnant, because we'd already got two other cats but we ended up keeping Tip's kittens as well.'

It seemed strange talking about something as ordinary as cats but Iain, at least, seemed quite interested, smiling at the kittens as they raced round his feet. Cate stood up and stretched, showing off her ultra flat stomach. She was right about being slimmer. Louise had never considered herself fat, or even slightly plump, but Cate was barely a size eight. No boobs to speak of, thin-faced, slightly androgynous but even so, even with the weight difference and the make-up and the clothes, there was no doubting the basic genes. But whose genes were they, could they be Dr Jay's genes, could Dr Jay be their biological mother? The mere thought made Louise want to throw up.

'Oh God,' said Louise again, as she looked at Cate. 'What am I going to tell my parents?'

'You're not going to tell them anything,' Cate said in her sharp, bossy way, 'because you won't be here.'

'What do you mean?'

'I mean that now you've seen me, you may as

well help with the rest of the puzzle. We're going on a little journey, there's someone we need to see.'

'Who, Dr Jay, you know where she is?'

'No, not her, not yet,' Cate said. 'We can talk about it on the way but you'll need an overnight bag.'

'I can't,' said Louise, cursing her voice that had gone all high-pitched and squeaky. 'I can't just go off like that! My parents will go mad if I just disappear.'

Parents – they were her parents, her biological parents! They had to be. Everything else, all the theories were just rubbish. Embarrassing, old and annoying her parents might be but they were hers, they'd always been hers and she loved them. Cate gave a huge, exaggerated sigh.

'Parents aren't difficult to fool. You call them and tell them you're staying with a friend. Then you phone them later to tell them what a lovely time you're having so they don't need to fret or check. And if it all goes well, I'll have you back here by tomorrow night, OK. If not, you just tell your parents you're staying at your friend's for a while longer. How simple is that?'

'Hang on,' said Iain. 'Where are we going? You never said anything about going anywhere else.'

'Well, I have now,' said Cate.

She turned to Louise.

'Now are you gonna pack or what?'

Without waiting for an answer, Cate told Iain to get the car, walked out of the kitchen, back towards the front door then headed up the stairs.

'Hey,' said Louise, following, 'why don't we just wait for my parents, ask them what's going on, find out what they know?'

'Tried that with mine,' said Cate, carrying on down the upstairs landing, 'and either your parents don't know very much, in which case there's no point asking or, like I said, they've been lying to you and they'll go on lying. Which is your room?'

Louise pushed open the door. Why did she do everything Cate asked, why didn't she stand up for herself? Because she couldn't, because all her energy had been drained, because all the certainties, everything she'd ever believed about her life was crumbling, falling apart and Cate was the one who seemed to have most of the answers even if she wasn't exactly sharing them all just yet.

Cate was wandering round the bedroom now, playing with the digi-frame, laughing at photos of Louise in her school uniform, looking at the mini-discs neatly filed in boxes on the shelves, while Louise pulled a bag from the cupboard and obediently started to pack.

'This is just about the tidiest bedroom I've ever seen,' said Cate, 'there's not even a cat hair lying around. You got some sort of obsessive compulsion or does the hired help clean up after you?'

'Neither,' said Louise, throwing some underwear into the bag. 'We have a daily help, of course.'

'Oh, of course, doesn't everyone?'

'Look can we cut the snide remarks and maybe just concentrate on getting this sorted out? You still haven't told me how you found me yet.'

'No I haven't, have I?'

'Only,' said Louise slowly, wondering how much to reveal, 'I think I might have seen you before.'

'At the baths, right, I wondered whether you'd seen us diving down behind the seats.'

Well at least that was one good thing. She hadn't imagined the blue car or the feeling of being followed, or being watched while she was swimming. She wasn't quite going down the Great-Aunt Mary route to madness; not just yet, anyway.

'No, not at the baths,' she said. 'It was about five years ago. I thought I'd sort of imagined it at the time but we saw each other . . .'

'Ah that,' said Cate, her eyes suddenly brighter, even more alert. 'Yes, well you're right, in a way. That's how I tracked you down but it's a bit more complicated than you think. I'm not sure you're ready for the full story just yet but I'll tell you before we get to Milton Keynes, I promise.'

'Milton Keynes!'

'That's where we're going, didn't I say?'

'But that's miles away.'

'Which is why you need an overnight bag – you got your toothbrush?'

Louise wandered into her bathroom, grabbed a few basics, came back and put them in her bag.

'Is that everything?' Cate asked.

'Yes but . . .'

'No buts,' said Cate, picking up the bag, 'just phone your parents and make it sound convincing.'

'I can't, I can't do this,' said Louise, stroking Tip who was now curled up on the end of the bed. 'It's mad.'

'Louise,' said Cate, managing to make the name sound like another of her long, exasperated sighs, 'please tell me you're not quite as dull and pathetic as you seem. Aren't you just a tiny, tiny bit curious about what's going on, wouldn't you like some answers?'

'Well yes but I still think there's a simple explanation.'

Cate laughed.

'There'll be an explanation, that's for sure,' she said. 'But it won't be simple. Wait till I tell you what else I've found out. It'll blow your head apart!'

6

Jessica quickened her pace. It made her headache even worse but the sooner she got home the sooner she could take some more paracetamol and lie down. God, it was so annoying. She hardly ever got headaches but she sure had one today. It had been building since mid afternoon, first a vague fuzziness, rising to a steady throb that she couldn't ignore.

'Probably a summer cold,' Emma had said.

'She's stressed 'cos she's missing Kal,' Beth had announced, with more than a hint of sarcasm.

'Bird flu,' Dan had added, pretending to choke and die.

'Might be the weather,' someone else had muttered.

That could be right. It was so bloody hot and muggy. Whatever the cause, she should have gone home as soon as the headache started but her mates had wanted to see the new 3D at the multi-plex. She didn't want to look like a total wimp so she'd gone. She'd even thought the pain might settle if her mind was occupied. It was only a stupid headache.

Stupid and very persistent – it just got worse and worse like her flaming head was going to explode. She was all set to go home straight after the film except when she'd turned on her com, there'd been the message from Mum asking her to call. It was all a bit weird. She'd expected Mum to be fretting about where she was, urging her not to be too late home but it was the opposite.

'Er, no, don't come back just yet,' Mum had said. 'Can you go back with one of your friends for a while? Jonathon's here. I need to talk to him.'

Banned from her own house – bloody great! She'd gone back to Dan's with the others. She'd have been OK if they'd all just chilled but no, everyone had livened up, started clowning around, being really loud. Thud, thud, thud, like someone was kicking a football round in her head so she'd decided to go home anyway, Jonathon or no Jonathon. She lived there not him – at least not yet. He might move in after he and Mum got married. Or Mum might sell up and move to Jonathon's. That's if they got married at all. It depended on whether Mum had wanted to be alone with him for the big romantic 'yes' or because she'd wanted to let him down quietly and gently.

Right at the moment, though, she really didn't care. She'd just sneak in quietly, go straight to her room and leave them to get on with whatever they were doing. She got her key out, walked quietly, carefully up the short path and let herself in. Straight away she heard Mum's raised voice coming from the lounge – not good news for poor Jonathon.

'I've told you,' Mum was saying. 'I'm not answering any more questions and no way am I letting you near my daughter. She's *my* daughter! She's got nothing to do with you now. You shouldn't have come here. I want you to go, right now.'

Jessica stopped at the foot of the stairs surprised that Mum was talking about her at all, let alone saying something like that to Jonathon. She waited for a moment replaying Mum's words, letting the evidence settle and, when it did, it was so obvious! It wasn't Jonathon in there, at all. Mum had lied.

There was only one person who Mum insisted she stay away from – Dad, it was Dad! Headache almost forgotten, Jessica hurled herself towards the door, pushed it open and burst in.

'Dad!'

But it wasn't Dad and it wasn't Jonathon either. The person getting up from the armchair was female, someone Jessica had seen before although not for a long time.

'Jessie,' Mum said, moving from her position near the TV to place herself between Jessica and the woman, 'er, this is er . . .'

'Jay,' said the woman, 'Dr Jay.'

'Yes, I know,' said Jessica, edging round Mum so she could see both of them clearly, see the unease on both their faces.

What she'd said about knowing Dr Jay wasn't quite true. Sure, she had a vague memory but she didn't really know her. Not as such, and she hadn't got a clue what was going on although it was obviously something private, secretive.

'Dr Jay was in the area,' Mum said, answering one of the unspoken questions that were swirling round Jessica's head. 'She thought she'd call in but she can't stay, she's just leaving.'

'So, how are you, Jessica?' Dr Jay asked, smiling

at her, staring as if she was taking in every detail, while Mum glared.

Jessica had never seen Mum look at anyone like that, not even Dad when things had been so cold between them.

'I'm fine,' said Jessica, as the steady thud in her temples started up again. 'I've got a bit of a headache, that's why I came home.'

'Oh,' said Dr Jay, sounding genuinely concerned, 'do you often get headaches?'

'No, she doesn't,' said Mum. 'Jessica's fine, like she said. I'll show you out.'

'It's all right,' said Dr Jay, 'I can manage. And you're sure everything's all right, Jessica?'

'She's sure,' Mum said, virtually pushing Dr Jay out of the room.

Jessica strained to hear the whispers out in the hall.

'I know how you feel,' Dr Jay was saying.

'No, you don't! You've got no idea, believe me.'

'But if you notice anything, if anyone gets in touch, you need to tell me, all right?'

'Get out,' Mum hissed, 'please just get out.'

The slam of the door ripped through Jessica's head. She had to do something about that bloody headache. She went through to the kitchen to get some tablets and when she returned to the lounge Mum was sitting on the sofa, head tilted back, legs outstretched, her face grey and strained.

'So what was that about?' Jessica asked. 'And don't tell me she was just passing. I heard you talking about me!'

'Well yes,' said Mum, sitting up a little straighter, 'she asked about you, she asked about the boys too. Why shouldn't she? She knew you all when you were little.'

Jessica sat down in the chair opposite Mum, searching back in her memories. She'd only seen the woman a few times before but she had the sort of striking, slightly too-perfect, slightly unnatural looks that were hard to forget. She'd vaguely remembered she was a doctor although the name had seemed wrong somehow. But it was hard to be sure of anything. It was ages since she'd last seen her. It must be years ago, before Dad left – but after Granddad had died. That was it! Dr Jay had been at Granddad's funeral – unless her memory had started playing tricks.

'Did she used to work with Granddad, or something?' Jessica asked.

'Er, for a short while, yes – only for a year or two, on and off, I think.'

But she was younger than Granddad, a lot younger – she was about her parents' age. Jessica looked at Mum, the creases in her forehead, the pure hatred that still clouded her eyes. Oh God, it all made sense! It was so obvious.

'It was her, wasn't it, she was the reason Dad left?'

A sound came from Mum's mouth, a cross between a shriek and a gasp, which told Jessica she was getting close.

'They were having an affair, weren't they?'

'Don't do this, Jessica,' Mum said, in a voice that was barely audible. 'It was a long time ago; it's all over, finished.'

Finished could mean anything, though. It could mean the affair was over or just that Mum didn't want to think about it, talk about it. No change there, then. Nobody wanted to talk about anything – that was the flaming problem. Ben and Alex had never mentioned anyone in Dad's life. It might mean they didn't know or, more likely, that they were in on the secret. So just her stuck on the outside then – typical!

But something was still well wrong. Whatever Dad's relationship was with Dr Jay, it was pretty weird her suddenly turning up, hassling Mum, gibbering on about someone getting in touch. There were enough flaming secrets in their family already without Dr Jay making it worse – so many things that didn't make sense. It was time to find a few answers but no way was Mum going to talk any more tonight.

Mum was looking down at her hands, twisting a ring round and round. It was a new ring! Jessica couldn't see it clearly but she could see which finger it was on. Mum had lied about Jonathon being here tonight, she'd lied about a lot of things, but clearly she'd seen Jonathon sometime today, possibly lunchtime, and given him an answer.

It didn't seem right to say congratulations or anything, not just yet, not now. Mum didn't exactly look like she was celebrating. She looked drained. Her shoulders were all tense, hunched, her eyes unusually dull. So instead of saying anything Jessica crossed over to the sofa. She sat down next to Mum, gave her hug, felt Mum's tears dripping onto her T-shirt and tried not to feel angry about the lies.

Louise hunched in the back of the tiny blue car. This was crazy; she should never have agreed to come. They could be kidnapping her, taking her anywhere and nobody would know. Her parents thought she was safe at Naomi's. Choosing Naomi was better than Gina, who lived too close, but her parents hadn't questioned it anyway, they had no reason to. They trusted her. The thing was – could she trust *them* any more? Could she even trust herself? Driving around the country like this, with a couple of strangers, was total madness but from the minute she'd seen Cate her brain had gone into free fall. She couldn't think straight, she barely knew what she was doing, let alone why.

Louise looked up as they passed a sign. They were definitely heading in the right direction, towards Milton Keynes, like Cate said, so that was good but Cate still hadn't explained why. They'd been driving for ages and, although Cate had asked a whole load of questions, talked a bit about her own life in Edinburgh and showed Louise some fairly boring pictures on her phone, she hadn't told them anything useful or said exactly where they were going or who they were going to see. Mercifully nothing yet that had fulfilled Cate's earlier warning and blown her head apart!

'You said you'd tell me,' Louise began, 'before we got to Milton Keynes.'

'And I will,' said Cate. 'We're gonna stop at some services soon, stay overnight at the motel.'

No consultation, no discussion, Cate was in charge, as ever. Iain had been pretty quiet, concentrating on the driving probably, but it was good just to know he was there. Iain was the reason she'd dismissed the kidnap theory, Iain was the reason she hadn't phoned the police or started screaming and banging on the windows demanding to be let out. Almost as soon as she'd realized he was nothing like the guy in her dream, she'd felt pretty safe with Iain.

'Cate,' she said, as memories of the nightmare flashed into her head, 'do you ever have dreams?'

'Sure, I guess, doesn't everyone?'

'Nightmares?'

'I dunno,' said Cate, as if she didn't much care either. 'I never remember dreams very well. Sometimes I wake up with this weird feeling that . . .'

'What?'

'Nothing! It's just a sort of disorientation thing, that's all, like I've been somewhere strange or I'm not quite myself – look, it doesn't matter, OK. I can't believe we're talking about frigging dreams.'

'Yes but do you ever have the same dream over and over? Because I . . .'

'Service sign,' said Cate, ignoring her as usual,

'last ones before Milton Keynes, we'll stop here. Not least 'cos I'm hungry and desperate for a pee.'

'Well, do you?' said Louise.

'What?'

'Have a recurring dream, only . . .'

'No,' said Cate, 'I don't have recurring dreams and I don't have special powers and I really, really don't think Dr Jay is an alien so forget all the spooky stuff, eh, and grow up!'

Louise felt herself blushing and hoped Iain couldn't see her through the rear-view mirror. Sharing her theories about Dr Jay's alien origins with Cate had been a big mistake. She'd only said it as a sort of joke, to try to explain just how creepy Dr Jay made her feel, but Cate had latched onto it, mocking like she'd mocked, ignored or dismissed about ninety per cent of the stuff Louise had talked about on the journey.

'Yeah, right, Lou, Dr Jay manufactured us on board a spaceship or shipped us in from Alpha Centauri to save a dying race.'

Well fine, she'd keep quiet from now on, let Cate do the talking and hope she came up with the information she'd promised. They turned into the services and, as soon as they stopped, Cate darted out.

'See you in the café,' she said.

It was the first time since seeing him on the drive that Louise had been with Iain on his own.

'So what do you think's going on?' she said as they headed across the car park, watching Cate disappear through the automatic doors.

'She's probably going to the loo. She said she was desperate.'

'I don't mean that! I mean us; me and Cate.'

'I don't know,' he said. 'I thought Cate was being a bit loopy, making it up or exaggerating the similarity till I saw you. And now with all the fertility stuff, well it's definitely odd.'

Iain was obviously a master of understatement!

'And Cate hasn't told you where we're going or anything?'

He shook his head, standing back slightly, letting her go through the doors first.

'Maybe she's found the clinic that did the treatment,' he said. 'She's got a whole folder of print-outs and stuff in that huge handbag thing she carries around.'

'So why isn't she telling us, why is she hiding stuff?'

'Oh, that's just Cate,' he said, 'she likes being mysterious, bit of a drama queen. She'll tell us in her own time, if there's anything much to tell. Come on, let's get something to eat.'

He got a salad for Cate, pizza for himself and sandwiches for Louise, which she struggled to eat.

'I'm sorry,' she said, 'I still feel a bit shaky.'

'Understandable,' said Iain.

'It's not just the look-alike thing,' said Louise. 'It's just that when you turned up it was so like the dream I tried to tell Cate about.'

'So you thought I was going to stab you?' Iain said when she told him about the nightmare. 'No wonder you fainted.'

'Cate thinks I'm a complete dozo.'

'Don't worry,' said Iain, stretching out his hand, lightly touching hers, 'she thinks the same about me too – and her parents! Cate thinks everyone's pretty dumb compared to her but maybe . . .'

'Glad to see you two are getting to know each other,' said Cate, suddenly appearing behind them.

Louise pulled her hand away from Iain although there was no reason to, nothing to feel guilty about.

'I've booked us two rooms,' Cate said, as she sat down. 'Me and Lou are sharing,' she added pointedly.

Jessica stared at the screen. She guessed there wouldn't be a reply to her message tonight but she carried on looking anyway. Her brothers would be working. They probably wouldn't pick up the message until tomorrow. Even when they did, they might not be able to tell her much. Or they might not want to. If they knew what had caused the break-up, if they knew about any affair, they sure hadn't mentioned it before. The headache had more or less gone so Jessica carried on idly messaging various friends, watching for anything popping up from her brothers. OK, so if no one was going to tell her anything, she'd just have to work it out for herself. It couldn't be that difficult. Think, think! The information was probably right there somewhere, in her head.

Before she could think of anything very much, a long message appeared from Kal, moaning about his shopping trip, his irritating cousins and all the wedding talk, ending with a question about her day, which she answered with a single word – *weird*. She was a bit stuck when he asked how weird. He knew the basics of her family set up but she wasn't sure she wanted to add too many gory details.

Ur not gonna believe this, she wrote, trying to keep it light, *but I had a visit from a freaky doctor! y? u not well?*

Whoops, she might have known it would lead to awkward questions. Still, it wouldn't do any harm to tell him a bit more. He might even be able to help. So she tapped in a fairly long reply explaining that Dr Jay wasn't an ordinary GP or quite freaky enough for a horror book.

just a bit odd for her to turn up after such a long time.

She paused then added the family connections, ending with her suspicions. Soon after sending she got a question back.

so u think she might be reason ur dad left?

Jessica answered but without giving too much detail. Just that Dr Jay used to work with Granddad. Keep it simple. No need to mention what kind of work. She wasn't quite sure how Kal felt about that kind of stuff. Some people could be funny about it.

so that's how ur dad wd have met her?

She answered with a simple yes. Kal might think it weird that Dad knew Granddad's work colleagues so well but it wasn't, not really. Dad was close to Granddad, he was always going round to see him. Their closeness seemed sort of natural. Gran had died when Dad was only four so it had always been just the two of them. Granddad had never remarried and there never seemed to be anyone special in his life.

'Your granddad's married to his work, a complete workaholic, a fanatic,' Mum used to say.

But then Mum had never exactly been a fan of Granddad's work. She made no big secret of that! She'd liked him as a person though, or at least it had seemed that way. Their arguments had been good-natured, nothing personal. And their relationship couldn't have been that bad because Granddad used to take time out, spend weekends with them or go on holidays with them sometimes, especially after he retired.

u never say much about ur G'dad

Kal was always talking about his grandparents but that was different. Both sets were still alive. He saw one lot almost every day and the others about once a month whereas she only saw Mum's parents, who lived on the Isle of Man, about twice a year and Dad's dad had been out of her life for ages now.

don't remember him too well, she wrote, *vague memories but not as many as I'd like. Can sort of picture the way he looked but that's more from photos and family films than memory*

His work, of course, she could look up in books

or on-line, and she often did because she liked all that sort of stuff and he was totally brilliant, one of the best in his field. If she could end up even half as clever as him she'd be well happy. So the work, yeah, but she wanted to stay off all that with Kal, and the rest, the personal stuff, was vague, like she'd said.

was only seven when he died, she added. *G'dad always closer to twins than me.*

Oh God, why was she getting into all this family stuff with Kal? It sounded sort of whingeing too but it was true enough. She definitely remembered a bit of a gender divide, a bit of a boys' club going on. Days on the beach with Dad, Granddad and the boys playing cricket and football – her and Mum building sandcastles or searching in rock pools for interesting shells, crinkly seaweed and tiny fishes.

Nothing unusual – there must have been dozens of families on the beach, split along similar lines, all playing out gender roles that weren't supposed to exist! And maybe, if Granddad had lived, they'd have grown closer as she got older 'cos she was way more interested in his work than the boys or anyone else in the family. No one else ever bothered to read his books or download any of his research.

'It's way out of my league,' Dad used to say, on the rare occasions he spoke about it at all.

The boys just weren't interested and Mum got all sniffy about it being an unethical waste of time and money! It would have been great to be able to talk to Granddad about it all now; now that she was older, now that she could understand most of it. But maybe she was fooling herself; maybe they wouldn't have grown any closer.

y u not close? Kal had asked, *y G'dad closer to ur brothers?*

Good questions. Maybe it was the gender thing or had Granddad kept his distance because she wasn't really part of him?

maybe cos I was adopted.

No, that was crazy. Why had she written that? She was heading down the wrong route completely. She never usually thought that way. Nobody had ever treated her differently. No one had ever made her feel that she was loved less than the boys, not ever, not even for a single minute.

FORGET THAT! she wrote – *was all down to G'dad that I was adopted in first place – he didn't have prob with it, no way.*

Neither had she until today! She never usually thought about it, let alone talked about it. Kal and

116

all her close mates knew, of course. She didn't hide it but it wasn't something she obsessed about. There was no point. She couldn't change anything, even if she wanted to. It wasn't like she'd ever known her birth parents – or that there was any chance of knowing them. She'd been with this family, her proper family, since she was just a few weeks old, although her exact age could only be guessed at. Sure the legal procedures took longer so she'd been almost two when the papers were finally signed but she'd never known any other life.

u think about all that much?

At any other time Jessica would have just said no to Kal's question but today she didn't.

sometimes – I sort of wonder who left me & why – but mainly no. No point – no clues so wouldn't be able to find out – anyway don't want to – this my real family.

She shook her head, wondering again why she was getting into all this with Kal, now of all times. She wasn't supposed to be thinking about herself, she should be thinking about Dr Jay; Dad and Dr Jay. She'd had an image of her earlier, dredged up from way back, a strong image of Dr Jay at the funeral, outside the crematorium. But there'd been so many people and it was so long ago it was hard to be sure, especially as she'd been so fixated on Dad that day. She'd barely noticed anything else. She'd never ever seen her dad like that before – crying, hardly able to stand, talk or function. Worse even than that awful day when the police had called round to tell them Granddad had been found by the lady who came in to clean for him.

Remembering what Dad had been like, how bad he'd been, she couldn't help wondering whether Dad had ever really got over it, ever accepted it. There was no way of knowing because they were never allowed to talk about it. Her eyes flicked to the screen as another message appeared from Kal. Still nothing from her brothers though.

will u ask ur dad bout dr jay?

not sure she replied.

She could hardly tell Kal that nobody ever answered questions in her family. Not the important ones anyway. It was mad. They were never allowed to talk about Granddad's death openly but she'd heard whispered conversations between her parents sometimes.

'I'm sure it wasn't deliberate,' Mum would say. 'It was an accident. He didn't mean to do it, I'm sure he didn't.'

Dad would snap some reply or just sit there

silently. But the point was – the point was that if Dr Jay was Granddad's colleague, if that's all she was, if she'd only worked with him for a short time, there'd been no reason to see her after Granddad died but they had seen her a couple of times, hadn't they, although never when Mum was around!

There was something else really odd too. She couldn't remember any references to Dr Jay when she'd read about Granddad's work. But maybe Dr Jay wasn't all that senior. Not everyone was mentioned by name. Anyway it didn't matter – it wasn't really her work she was interested in. She suddenly sat up straighter. There was another message from Kal but she ignored it for the moment because there was something from her brothers.

'What's with the late-night questions? You turning into an insomniac or what? Don't think Dad was up to anything with Dr J or anyone else. Just friends that's all. Nothing caused the break-up. It just happened. Chill,

xx A&B

It just happened! Thanks, Ben; thanks, Alex, very enlightening! 'Just friends' could mean absolutely anything. It could mean they used to know each other vaguely, casually or that they were still in touch and very, very friendly! Except that it didn't make sense. If they were involved there was no real reason for Dad to hide it. Loads of marriages split up; loads of people had affairs, so there shouldn't be any big deal about Dad and Dr Jay.

They could have just told the truth. Knowing why Dad left would have made it easier in a way – for all of them. So there must be some sort of reason for the secrecy. There was something she was missing. She just had to think it out logically, like it was a science experiment or something. Logic was what she was good at – most of the time.

She glanced again at the screen. The boys had ignored her questions about Granddad completely so she asked again, sat up for ages, chatting to Kal about nothing in particular, thinking about Dad and waiting for the reply from her brothers that never came.

7

Louise sat on the edge of one of the beds, Iain lay stretched out on the other, half-asleep, while Cate set up her micro-comp on the small table and pulled a folder from her bag. It had been weird walking through the service station with Cate. People hadn't stared exactly but Louise had sensed them looking.

Did twins always attract that sort of attention or was it because she and Cate managed to be so alike yet different at the same time? And with Cate looking so much older, people might have thought they were sisters rather than twins; sisters who looked incredibly similar. Or maybe people hadn't been looking at them at all. It could have been her imagination on overdrive again. In fact, with any luck this whole thing would turn out to be imaginary or a nightmare that she'd wake up from soon!

When they'd got to their rooms, Cate typically

hadn't exactly been in a hurry to share her information or the next stage of her plan. She'd insisted on having a shower first, which seemed to last for ever, then she'd borrowed some money from Iain and gone off to buy drinks, laughing when Louise had said she only wanted sparkling water.

'Wouldn't it be better if Iain went?' Louise had asked. 'You might not get served.'

'Fake i.d.,' Cate had said, waving a card at Louise, 'but they won't ask.'

Cate's shower and drinks hunt had given Louise another forty minutes on her own with Iain. She'd deliberately avoided talk of herself or Cate, all the weird look-alike stuff, and asked questions about him instead. It was easier than she'd thought, talking to Iain. Usually she wasn't good at talking to lads. It wasn't something she'd ever admit to Cate but she hardly knew any boys and she'd never had a real boyfriend. Thanks to her parents sending her to an all girls' school, boys were a bit of an alien species and the ones she'd met when she'd been out with her friends, she hadn't much liked.

Iain was different though, maybe because he was older than the few lads she knew. He was twenty-one, he said. She'd found out, amongst other things, that he was from the north-west of Scotland, up near Fort William, wherever that was, that he was a keen skier, was studying history at university, that he had an older sister who was married with two kids and that his parents ran a B&B. All fairly normal, reassuring stuff and he was sort of different when he wasn't around Cate; more talkative, more natural and confident.

He hadn't said anything about Cate, about how they'd got together or why he'd chosen her rather than any of the girls at university but Louise had got the impression that it was the other way round; that Cate had chosen him. It seemed natural that Cate would go for older guys and it wasn't hard to believe that Cate always got what she wanted. Louise could see why Iain, or any other lad, whatever their age, would be attracted to Cate. It was funny that. She could see that Cate was pretty stunning yet she'd never thought of herself as more than passable. Was it all a matter of attitude and confidence, could she be more like Cate if she wanted to?

When Cate got back with the drinks, she announced that she'd contacted her parents again and insisted Louise did the same. Louise didn't know what kind of reply Cate had got but her own parents had just said to have a nice time. Wonderful, yes – sitting around a motel room waiting for Cate to let them in on her little or not-so-little secrets!

Clearly Cate was a late-night sort of person, revived by the shower and the drinks, unlike Louise who was totally knackered. Now, finally, Cate was almost ready. Probably the information wasn't even going to be worth knowing. More likely it was Cate over-dramatizing, making it all seem even stranger than it was. Why, Louise wondered, for about the millionth time, had she ever agreed to this, why hadn't she stayed at home and tried to talk to her parents? Despite what Cate had said, there was probably some really simple explanation.

'Shit,' Cate suddenly said, staring at the micro-screen.

'What?' said Louise, getting up off the bed.

'What I wanted to show you isn't there any more.'

Oh, right, what a surprise! Was there ever anything to show?

'Never mind,' Cate was saying, 'I've got print-outs and this'll do to start with. OK, you ready for this?'

'I don't know until I see it,' Louise muttered.

Iain, probably jolted awake by Cate's initial shriek, got up off the bed and followed Louise towards the table. Cate pushed her chair back, allowing them full view of the small screen. Louise stared at the picture. There were words on the screen too but they were tiny and they wouldn't quite come into focus because already Louise was starting to feel slightly faint, slightly dizzy, her eyes blurring.

'This is one of your network sites, right?'

Even as she said it, a chill swept through her body because the girl in the picture looked even more like her than Cate did, if that was possible. This girl's face wasn't quite as thin as Cate's. She wasn't wearing any make-up, or at least, not much. Her hair was a bit shorter and rather lighter than Louise's but much longer than Cate's. The eyes, of course, were blue; that exact shade of blue.

'No,' said Cate, stretching out her hand, scrolling down, 'this bundle of crap is one of Jessica's web-pages, Jessica who lives in Milton Keynes.'

Louise backed towards the bed and sat down again, looking at Iain who came to stand beside her. It was clear he didn't know. He wasn't in on this; he'd never heard of or seen this Jessica before.

'Bloody hell!' Iain said.

'I told you it was very, very freaky,' said Cate, turning to face them.

'*You've* made this page,' said Louise. 'This is one of your little jokes, yes?'

Images could be changed. It wouldn't have been difficult for Cate to do this, would it, but then why should she, unless this was all one big, crazy hoax?

'I wish I had made it up,' said Cate, 'but no, it's for real. I found Jessica first, totally by accident a while back and maybe, just maybe, I wouldn't have thought much of it, except for this.'

She pulled a print-out from her purple, plastic wallet folder and passed it to them.

'It's a ghost story that Jessica posted,' she said. 'Recognize it?'

Louise didn't recognize it, as such, but she knew the basic story. They'd talked about it back at the house when Cate had been typically evasive.

'*I think I might have seen you before. About five years ago. I thought I'd sort of imagined it at the time but we saw each other, didn't we?*'

'*Ah that. Yes, well you're right, in a way. That's how I tracked you down but it's a bit more complicated than you think.*'

'You've made it up,' Louise insisted. 'You've made Jessica up. It isn't true, it was you I saw at the museum, it must have been,' she added, as Iain took the print-out from her, clearly trying to catch up on a story where he was several stages behind.

'I've never even been to London, let alone the Science Museum,' said Cate, 'but you don't have to believe that. What was she wearing, the girl you saw?'

'A sort of uniform, dark blue sweatshirt, I think, with a logo. I'm not sure, I was looking mainly at her face but I honestly thought I'd imagined the similarity. That's why I never told anyone, I thought I'd imagined it!'

'But it was definitely a uniform she was wearing, a school uniform?'

'Yes. I saw her rush back to her group then I caught up with my class who were already by the door and we left shortly afterwards to go to the National Gallery so . . .'

'Cate's never been to school,' Iain said, 'and I don't think she'd be seen dead in any sort of uniform.'

'But you've been to school, haven't you, Louise?' said Cate. 'Jessica gave a great description of the ghost's uniform, don't you think? I mean, how many schools still insist on a get-up like that? No wonder she thought it was 1950s. Straw boater with a maroon ribbon for Christ's sake! Hardly your bog-standard junior so it was easy enough to find.'

Everything devious seemed easy, according to Cate!

'I just checked out all the ultra-mega-posh expensive prep schools,' she was saying. 'It took a while 'cos I made the mistake of starting with London schools but hey I found it eventually. Then all I had to do was track down the nearest private senior school and there you were, quite the little star with all your volleyball and swimming trophies.'

'So it was Jessica I saw at the museum and you found me through her,' Louise mumbled. 'Jessica's real, she exists.'

'Yes,' said Cate, 'unlike the tooth fairy or Father Christmas, she exists. So now that we all believe in Jessica, can we move on a bit?'

'Hang on,' said Louise, 'if this is true, why did you let me go on about twins back at the house, when you knew there were three of us?'

'I didn't want to give you information overload,' said Cate, 'especially as you were having trouble with just the two of us. But twins, triplets, the same ideas apply though I reckon the Cuckoo Theory's got the edge over the Omen Theory, don't you?'

'I feel sick,' said Louise.

'Yeah, it got me a bit that way,' said Cate. 'I mean, twins is one thing but three of us? Identical triplets are pretty rare. I checked. Depending on whose stats you use, triplets occur in about one in every six thousand births. But not all those are identical. You can get fraternals like you can with twins.'

'What's the difference?' said Iain.

'Duh, didn't you do biology or what? Fraternal means when two or more eggs are produced, identical is when an egg splits,' Cate explained. 'And they're more likely to split when fertility treatment is involved so we're sort of back to that again.'

'So could someone do that deliberately?' Iain said. 'I'm not sure why they'd want to but could they split an egg after fertilization then implant the two or three parts into different people?'

'Yeah, I reckon,' said Cate. 'Maybe the egg split naturally during the fertility process, maybe not.'

'So what about quads,' said Louise. 'How rare are quads?'

'Pretty rare, I guess,' said Cate, 'even with fertility treatment. Why, don't you think three of us are bizarre enough? Shall we try and find another? And why stop at four, how about octuplets? Let's go for eight, shall we?'

There was something even edgier about Cate's voice than usual, as if she really feared there might be large numbers of them around somewhere.

'It's not a random guess,' said Louise. 'I think I might already have found a fourth. I've been trying to tell you. Yesterday, at my check-up, Dr Jay called me Katherine by mistake. So maybe Katherine's another patient, maybe she looks like us.'

'Shit,' said Cate, 'you were right! Dr Jay's got a machine on her spaceship, churning out multiple copies. Maybe we're androids, not people, an updated version of those Japanese robots – they look pretty realistic. Have you checked yourself out for metal bits? Anybody got a magnet?'

'Will you stop taking the piss out of everything I say?'

'I'm not,' said Cate. 'Well, OK, maybe a bit. But I really don't think there can be four of us.'

'Why not?' said Iain. 'If there's definitely three . . .'

'That's right,' said Cate, standing up, 'there's definitely three – anything else is guesswork. So let's stick to what we know for now, let's stick to the three of us.'

Iain sat down on the vacated chair, facing Louise, while Cate paced and talked.

'Right,' she said, 'so let's say we're identical triplets but carried by different mothers – some sort of social experiment, nature versus nurture and all that! Maybe we're being secretly filmed, like in *The Truman Show*.'

'Good film,' said Iain, 'we watched it in school once.'

'Guy called Truman,' Cate explained to Louise, 'thinks he's living a normal life but he's actually being brought up on a film set.'

'And everything he does is broadcast live as a sort of docu-soap,' Iain added.

'Yes, I know, I've seen it,' said Louise, wondering where Cate's obsession with films was getting them.

'I mean I'm not saying we're going live to the nation or anything,' said Cate, 'but we could be part of a study.'

She didn't sound sure, somehow, as though she was desperately trying to grasp at something relatively sane.

'I mean, that's what we've always been told,' said Cate, 'that we were part of a study. I'd always thought it was all boring and technical and academic but maybe it's not, maybe it's more of a social study.'

'That can't be right,' said Louise. 'Doctors aren't

allowed to mess around like that. They couldn't split up triplets just so they could study the bloody social effects. There are rules about that sort of stuff and I don't know about your parents but mine would never agree to it.'

'I don't think Tess and Carla would either,' said Iain.

'You hardly bloody know them,' Cate snapped. 'You don't know what they'd do. People can get pretty desperate for babies – agree to almost anything.'

'But it doesn't make sense,' said Iain.

'Iain's doing a degree in stating-the-bloody-obvious,' said Cate. 'We know it doesn't make sense, Iain. That's why we're trying to sort it out and I think Jessica might be the key.'

'Dr Jay looks like the key to me,' said Louise.

'Yeah but I can't find out anything about her,' said Cate, 'mainly because that's not her real name.'

'How do you know?' Louise asked.

'Because I once heard Tess call her Faye and nobody, but nobody, calls their kid Faye Jay, do they?'

'They might. People have called their kids weirder names and anyway Jay could be her married name.'

'It could be but I don't think she's married so I'm guessing it's an initial, J for Jones or Johnson or Jekyll or something.'

'I thought we weren't doing guesswork,' said Iain.

'All right, smart-arse,' Cate snapped, 'we're not and thinking about Dr Jay doesn't get us anywhere, whereas Jessica . . .' Cate paused as she picked up the folder and pulled out two more sheets of paper. 'Jessica gives us lots of clues. Trouble is, they cause more problems than they solve.'

'Why?' Louise asked.

'Well, Jessica's not quite like us,' said Cate, looking at her sheets of paper. 'Her parents aren't same sex, they're not particularly old and they've got other kids – so not obvious candidates for fertility treatment, you'd say.'

'OK,' said Louise, the sickness intensifying, 'so do you think they might be the original parents, Jessica's and ours? But if Jessica's parents were our parents,' she added, 'how the heck did Dr Jay get them to part with an egg or thirds of an egg in the first place, unless they were sort of tricked into it?'

'I don't think that's the way round it was,' said Cate, 'because they're not even Jessica's birth parents – Jessica's adopted. I don't know when, how or why because she doesn't make a big deal of it but she's mentioned it.'

'So were her brothers or sisters adopted?' Louise asked. 'You said there were other kids.'

'Brothers,' said Cate, 'she's got older twin brothers.'

'Twins?' said Louise.

'Yeah,' said Cate. 'I told you it got complicated. I don't think they were adopted but they're identical. The plot thickens, eh? Maybe there's another half dozen or so of them around somewhere.'

'So if Jessica's adopted,' said Louise, 'who's her birth mother? Could your mum or mine have had twins and given one away or what?'

Cate didn't answer. She picked up the 'ghost' story that Iain had left on the bed, put it with the other papers she was holding and flipped through them.

'So what are you planning to do now?' Iain asked. 'Go and see this Jessica, scare her half to death like you frightened Louise?'

'Me,' said Cate, 'it wasn't me who leapt out at her.'

'He didn't leap,' said Louise, 'and I only fainted because it was so like my nightmare.'

Cate narrowed her eyes, as if mention of the

nightmare was new, as if she'd forgotten the conversation in the car.

'It's nothing,' said Louise, knowing Cate would find something to mock.

'She's jogging through a park,' said Iain, 'and this guy steps out from behind a tree and stabs her. So when she saw me she freaked a bit.'

Cate's eyes narrowed even more, she looked puzzled for a moment, then her face relaxed and she half-smiled.

'That actually happened to a friend of Tess and Carla's,' said Cate, as if she was talking about something ordinary, something totally normal. 'Well, I don't know whether she was jogging or not but she got stabbed to death in a park.'

'Are you making this up?' said Louise.

'According to you, I make everything up but, no, it really happened.'

'How?' said Louise. 'I mean why? Who was she, who killed her?'

'Dunno,' said Cate, 'it happened ages ago, before I was born, probably. I just remember Carla talking about it once. I was only young, I think, 'cos I remember Tess shutting her up in that not-in-front-of-the-children sort of way.'

Cate's eyes had done that narrowing thing

again, as if she was thinking, searching for something in the back of her mind. When the eyes opened properly, after a second or so, they looked worried, as if they'd seen something lurking in Cate's subconscious that they hadn't really wanted to see. Louise couldn't blame them – she imagined Cate's subconscious could be a pretty scary place.

'It's sort of weird though,' said Louise, before she could stop herself, 'that I dream about something that actually happened to your mums' friend.'

'Oooooh, spooky,' said Cate, her eyes returning to their normal lively, mocking state, 'thought transference and all that. Get real, Lou. Someone gets stabbed nearly every day and I bet it's one of the most common dreams, after falling and drowning. It's probably about sex – most dreams are. I'll check it out for you sometime, I know a great dream site, but right now could we get back to Jessica. There isn't really an easy way to do it but I've got a plan.'

'I don't suppose this plan involves anything remotely sensible does it,' Iain said, 'like going to the police or the medical council or at least back to your parents with what you've found out so far?'

'Yes and no,' said Cate. 'Yes, it's as sensible as I can manage under the circumstances and no, we're not reporting it to anybody just yet. Not least because I think Jessica should have a say in what we do next.'

Louise glanced across at Iain who raised his eyebrows slightly. Was he thinking the same as her? That Cate wasn't exactly big on consultation so why should she be bothered about Jessica's opinion?

'It's still possible,' said Cate, as though she was desperately trying to convince herself, 'that there's some sort of half-reasonable explanation, that there's nothing particularly sinister going on so I reckon we should keep our options open for now. But we need to get it sorted pretty quickly.'

'Why,' said Louise, 'why the sudden urgency?'

'It's not sudden,' said Cate. 'It was always part of the plan. My next appointment with Dr Jay is on Monday. So if we need to see her, as I suspect we will, that's our chance, isn't it?'

As she spoke, Cate carefully put her print-outs back in the folder, filing them somewhere near the front of a bundle of papers, before putting the folder back in her bag.

'What else have you got in there?' Louise asked.

'Make-up, hairbrush, purse, the usual sort of thing people keep in bags.'

'Not in the bag,' said Louise, although Cate obviously knew what she'd meant. 'In the folder.'

'Oh that's just background stuff, print-outs from your web pages, more of Jessica's, nothing really important.'

'Can I see?'

'Not now, it's late. I'll show you tomorrow, if you insist.'

Cate tucked the bag down by the side of one of the beds. More secrets, more mysteries! Louise knew Cate had no intention of telling her the Jessica plan or showing her what else was in the folder. Well, OK, she didn't have to wait for Cate to show her, did she? She was sick of Cate dictating every move. She'd watch, wait for her chance – maybe later tonight when Cate was asleep.

8

Dr Jay kicked off her shoes as soon as she got to her hotel room and sat down in the armchair in the far corner. She took a notepad and pen out of her handbag and started jotting down notes as she often did as she was thinking. There was something about the flow of words on a page that helped her get her ideas straight.

Meeting with Jessica's mother went as badly as expected. She's too emotional. Not the type to forgive or forget! Clever enough — in a wishy-washy liberal sort of way — but definitely not what you'd call rational or logical. Doesn't respond to REASON — I've never ever been able to make her see sense. Don't know what made me think I could manage it today. She's blindly unreasonable where Jessica's concerned. On the other hand — she's no liar — except with her daughter, of course. SO — if she said there's been nothing odd happening, no unusual visitors, then there hasn't been.

She stopped writing for a moment, letting her pen draw neat swirls along the edge of the paper as she thought, until the swirls became writing again.

Possibilities:

Cate's investigations haven't taken her in that direction.

Jessica's mother is lying.

Cate's contacted Jessica but Jessica hasn't told her mum.

The latter was possible. Jessica had seemed a bit tense, with the headache and everything. Pity she hadn't been able to snatch a few words with Jessica on her own. Her pen etched a few more random swirls then wrote the words:

Next steps:

Go back tomorrow — try to catch Jessica alone?

That's why she'd decided to stay the night in Milton Keynes, after all; to keep her options open.

Advantages:

Jessica is easiest one to talk to. She's the one who might understand.

I'd really like to see Jessica again anyway, just to talk to her, spend some time with her.

She crossed out the last point. She couldn't allow sentiment to get in the way, not now. She looked back to where she'd written *Next steps* and squeezed in the words *phone Cate*. Perhaps clever, curious Cate was the one to focus on.

Dr Jay got up and opened her bag that was on the bed. She had a couple of spare phones and coms that could be used then discarded if necessary. She needn't be specific. She could just say Tess and Carla were worried, which was true, of course. She picked out one of the phones and sat down again. No, it was no good. Cate wouldn't even answer a call from an unknown number, she'd be far too cautious for that. And if she did, it would only make her more suspicious, more wary. Not a good idea at this stage. It was best that Cate didn't know she'd been in contact with Carla and Tess.

It was so frustrating! She abandoned the phone and picked up the pen again.

I really need to know what Cate's up to. What does she know? How much has she found out? It would help if Tess and Carla were being completely straight with me but they're not. They were acting strange when I saw them so they're definitely holding back on something.

You didn't need to be a genius to work that one out!

So — I can't trust them. Can't trust anyone.

Worst case scenario: If people find out I can change my identity again and disappear — completely this time. No problems, everything already in place.

Her pen hovered over the notepad. Yes, she could disappear, take the easy way out, but she wasn't sure that was what she wanted any more.

I'm sick of hiding, sick of covering up and besides —

More swirls appeared round the edges of the pad.

I owe the girls more than that. I always meant to tell them sometime when they were old enough

*to understand. Maybe now is the time. Maybe
I can make them understand or even appreciate
what we did for them. Only it wasn't really for
them, of course.*

The swirls, each time she paused, were getting thicker, blacker.

*Be honest – I did it for myself! For ME. I had
to. But it wasn't wrong.*

She sat back in her chair, chewing the end of the pen. Selfish, yes, illegal certainly, but not wrong, no one would ever convince her it was wrong. The tricky bit though was convincing people it was right – the girls, the public, the media, the law. People could be so reactionary, so entrenched, so reluctant to embrace progress! There'd always been protests against advancements. She jabbed the pen down on the paper then started making a list, writing rapidly.

*Anaesthetics during childbirth
Smallpox vaccine
MMR
Organ transplants
Stem cell research*

Within minutes she'd filled the page and turned over, adding to her list in no particular order. It didn't matter what century you delved into, you'd always find reactionaries.

Galileo – condemned by the church
Darwin – some nutters still deny evolution!

It was unbelievable; even now you got the anti-science brigade sending death threats to scientists, trying to blow up research facilities. And the press didn't help with their sensationalism, hyping everything up just to sell a few extra copies.

BUT she wrote in large letters to remind herself science always wins out in the end. It has to. It's the only thing, in a chaotic world, that makes any sense! So it's time to admit what I've done, to stand up for what I believe in, make the world embrace the possibilities – whether people like it or not!

She put the pen and pad down, stretched out her wrist, looked at her i-com, then at the phone resting on the arm of the chair. She had a couple of calls to make, a few things she needed to check before she made her final decision but it was too late to be calling people now. It would have to wait until the morning.

Louise lay awake listening to Cate's steady breathing that seemed to suggest she was asleep at last. They'd been in bed for about four hours but for the first three Cate had sat up with her micro. Louise had tried to talk, to show an interest, but Cate had turned the small screen away and snapped out her usual short, less than enlightening, answers.

'There's stuff I need to look up.'

'What kind of stuff?'

'Just stuff, that's all.'

Judging by all the huffs, sighs and muttered swear words, Cate wasn't having too much luck but she obviously didn't want any help so eventually Louise had given up and pretended to sleep. She might even have dozed a little because, although she hadn't been aware of any change, any movement, she suddenly realized the micro and the bedside light had been switched off and that Cate had, apparently, settled down.

Louise rolled towards the edge of her bed and peered over at Cate. She wanted to be sure she was fully asleep before she made her move. Was now the time? It wasn't totally dark. There was enough light to see where she was going, to be able to find the folder, but not enough to read by and she couldn't risk the bedside light or even the faint light from her com. So she'd have to take the folder into the bathroom – if she could get it without waking Cate. She gently eased back the bed covers and got out of bed.

She wasn't sure why she was so worried about Cate waking, except that she wanted to see what was in that folder and she wanted to see it now, tonight. She didn't want Cate to stop her, as she surely would if she woke up. There was no movement from Cate though, no change in the breathing pattern so she began to edge towards Cate's bed.

It was a bit like that silly game they used to play in PE when they were kids. The one where someone stood, facing the wall, with one hand behind their back while everyone else tried to creep up. There were variations; sometimes you had to tap the person on the hand, sometimes you had to pick up a tin of small stones without it rattling, giving away your position. The person at the wall wasn't allowed to turn round but if they pointed in your direction you were out. Louise had been a good pointer but a completely hopeless creeper.

Creeping round the motel room in her bare feet

on the soft carpet was easier. She just had to make sure she didn't bump into anything, tread on the micro that Cate had left on the floor or drop the folder as she tried to lift it from beside the bed. She kept her breathing soft as she approached, in case Cate heard it or felt it, but Cate slept on.

The instinct was to hurry once you'd got the tin of stones or, in this case, the folder but you had to stop yourself; retrace your steps quietly. Clutching the surprisingly heavy folder, she headed for the bathroom. The door was half open so slithering in was easy but if she put the light on, the extractor would start whirring. Was that enough to wake Cate, was she a light sleeper? Best not to risk it, it was best to use the com light.

Louise sat down on the cold tiled floor, took the com off her wrist, positioned the light, opened the folder and lifted out the thick bundle of papers. Cate had filed the Jessica printouts back carefully so there was obviously an order that she needed to keep to so Cate wouldn't know she'd been rummaging. Why, why was she being so careful, why was she so bloody scared of Cate?

Louise put the papers face up on the floor. The first ones were taken from her own and her parents' web pages so nothing new or interesting there, apart from a few handwritten annotations. How had Cate tracked down some of this stuff? She'd even drawn a little family tree for heaven's sake, with both sets of Louise's grandparents, who'd all died at around the same time, eight years ago, victims of old age and the flu epidemic.

But it wasn't so much what the annotations said as the precision of the handwriting that caught Louise's attention. It was small, almost as small as the printed font, incredibly neat, not what she'd expected Cate's writing to be like and certainly nothing like her own large, curly loops. She turned the pages carefully putting each of them face down, ready to be gathered up and replaced in order.

The next batch was all about Jessica and, like with some of her own pages, there were additional notes. Cate had written in Jessica's address and home phone number. How did she find out that sort of stuff? Some sections had been highlighted in different colours, as though there was some sort of code although Louise couldn't make out what it was. Maybe she'd come back to it when she'd flipped through the rest.

Cate had certainly been busy. It looked like she'd checked out every possible angle, every possible connection, however weird. There were pages on the films Cate had quoted – *The Truman Show*, *The Omen* and a few more besides. There were some tightly printed, technical notes on fertility treatment that Louise couldn't understand then something a little easier; a copy of a newspaper article from ages back, before they were born. An American woman had usable eggs but was unable to carry a baby, so her own mother had, at the age of sixty-one, become a surrogate carrier thus giving birth to her own grandchild! How yucky was that?

There were other articles as well, dozens of them. Cases from all over the world, cases of older parents, same sex parents, multiple births and even someone who'd used the frozen sperm of her dead husband to give birth to fraternal twins. Cate was right, the technology was all there, it had been for decades, and it seemed there was nothing, but nothing, people wouldn't do to have a baby. It also seemed that whatever you wanted done, however bizarre, however unethical or illegal, there was someone, somewhere prepared to carry out the procedure.

So why hadn't Cate shared this information, let them read it on the journey down or something? It was all interesting, a lot of it well-weird, but nothing to be secretive about. Louise was just about to turn to the next page when she heard a noise. Someone was moving about. She froze, the piece of paper clutched in her hand, waiting for Cate to appear at the doorway, scowling, snapping and snarling.

Instead she heard a door, another door, quietly opening and closing; maybe the person in the next room getting up to go to the loo or some guest departing mega-early. It wasn't Cate moving around but it might be soon, it was almost five o'clock already. Strangely, having been absolutely knack-ered earlier, she wasn't tired any more.

Louise started to flip through the papers a bit quicker. It was mainly more of the same then suddenly a picture of a mouse. Mice, what had mice got to do with anything? Early fertility experiments maybe? She shuddered, partly because the cold from the tiles was starting to seep through right to her bones and partly because she hated the idea of animal experiments. Animals kept in cages, in laboratories, having organs taken out, body parts added on, brains tampered with, diseases deliber-ately injected into them and medicines tested on them.

A picture of Tip and her other cats flashed into her mind. They were sentient, they felt pain and they had feelings. She could barely believe that someone could just torture animals in the name of science. She'd never thought about it before but the fertility treatment that had, allegedly, produced her would have been tried on animals first, wouldn't it? Did she owe her life to families, generations of suffering mice?

Only these mice, Cate's mice, hadn't been used in fertility treatment as such. She turned to the next page and the next; from mice to macaques with half a dozen animals in between. Details of experiments highlighted in bright, luminous orange with Cate's neat handwritten notes beside them. Was Cate serious, was Cate really looking for answers here? This was the sort of paranoid fantasyland she herself might stray into, in fact she'd given it more than a passing thought already, but she hadn't dared mention it to Cate. Cate would just laugh at this sort of thing or set off on one of her sarcastic rants.

Louise sat, still shivering, with pages spread out in front of her. She knew it went on, of course. It was so common with animals it barely made the news any more and, when it did, she didn't like to watch. She didn't really want to know. It was bad enough with animals, but people! No, no way, it was sick, totally sick. Why had Cate included this stuff? Cate couldn't really believe this applied to them, any more than she believed that three babies had been murdered, Omen-style, and replaced by demon triplets, except . . .

There'd been something highlighted in Cate's notes on Jessica. She hadn't stopped to read it properly but it had caught her attention because it had been the only page marked in bright orange; all the rest had been pink, blue and green. She started flipping back through the pages, not bothering with neatness or order any more. Cate had said something about Jessica being the key but maybe she didn't mean Jessica exactly, maybe she meant Jessica's granddad!

Louise pulled out the orange notes, reading them carefully this time, pains starting to rip across her stomach as she read. It was stomach cramp that's all, the way she'd been sitting, cross-legged, hunched over the papers but, as she straightened her legs, the nausea gushed up. She just managed to lurch towards the loo before she threw up.

Jessica glanced at the clock as she stretched out and picked up her com from the bedside table, wondering who'd be phoning her this early on a

Friday morning in the hols; not Kal or any of her friends that was for sure! A quick glance gave her the answer.

'Hi, Jess, you OK?'

'Hi, Alex.'

'It's Ben.'

Oh well, easy mistake to make, they sounded the same and used each other's coms all the time!

'Can't talk long,' Ben was saying, 'we're on early shift. That's why I didn't call last night – needed a few hours' sleep. I was knackered, still am. Anyway, what's wrong?'

'Nothing,' said Jessica, sitting up properly.

'So why all the questions?'

She hesitated. She shouldn't tell them about Mum and Jonathon. Besides that wasn't really what had got her started on all this. It was more to do with Dr Jay's visit.

'Mum was a bit upset last night,' she said, trying to remember exactly what she'd told them on-line. 'It got me thinking about Dad, that's all.'

'And Granddad?'

'Yeah, him too, I was looking for connections, I guess, wondering if Dad ever really got over it.'

She let her voice drop to a whisper as she heard Mum's bedroom door opening. Mum was up early.

She was going to work today so she'd be leaving soon. She never bothered with breakfast or anything on office days. A brisk walk to work with an orange juice and a banana when she got there was all part of her ongoing keep-fit campaign.

'I mean, Mum never tells me anything.'

'I'm not sure there's anything to tell,' said Ben. 'I think it was just accidental overdose, like the coroner said. I know Dad felt guilty. I reckon he still does but . . .'

'Guilty, why?' she said, still keeping her voice low even though she'd heard Mum going downstairs.

'About the row,' Ben said, as if it was common knowledge, as if it was something Jessica ought to know.

'What row?'

'They had a row, just before Granddad died.'

'What about?'

'I don't know. Dad never said, not even to Mum, I reckon. It probably wasn't much. But you know how it is when your last words to someone weren't – good.'

Jessica didn't know. She had no idea how it must feel but she was beginning to understand why Dad had taken it so very badly.

'Look, Jess, I'm sorry, I gotta go. I'm late. Alex is waiting. Talk later, eh?'

'Yeah, thanks, Ben.'

She fastened her com onto her wrist and got out of bed, wondering whether Dad's row with Granddad had been trivial, a stupid, throwaway comment or whether it had been about something important. Maybe Granddad had found out about Dad's affair with Dr Jay. It was possible but then the argument could have been about anything; anything at all. Maybe the affair hadn't even been going on back then, perhaps it had started after Granddad died.

That was more likely, in a way; that the affair had started sometime in the five years between Granddad dying and her parents splitting up. And whatever the row had been about, it surely hadn't caused Granddad to kill himself. It was like Ben and the coroner said. It was accidental. It had to be; a combination of the drink and the painkillers Granddad had been taking. The argument, of course, might have caused him to drink more than usual, to be careless. Granddad, as far as she remembered, hadn't been a heavy drinker, not the type to sit drinking whisky on his own, but whisky had definitely been involved that night. The glass and the empty bottle had been on his desk when he was found. The alcohol levels in his blood suggesting that the bottle had been full at the start of his binge.

He must have been mega-stressed to drink like that but from the bits Mum had said, Granddad just wasn't the type to crack under pressure. He couldn't have been! There'd been demos, protests against his work, all through his career but he hadn't let them get to him. Even the 'Frankenstein' jibes in the press, after one of his early projects had gone spectacularly wrong, and that letter bomb hadn't worried him too much, according to Mum. Or maybe they had. He'd retired early, when she was very young, so maybe it had all started to get to him. The row with Dad, whatever it had been about, could have just tipped him over the edge.

'Jessie, I'm off now,' Mum called up.

Jessica darted out of her room and ran downstairs. Mum was by the front door, in her smart grey work suit, hunting through her handbag, checking she'd got everything, as she always did before leaving the house.

'Mum,' Jessica began.

Her mum looked up. She was still looking tired and strained, her usually fresh-looking skin almost as grey as the suit. Now wasn't the time for questions, not the questions Jessica wanted to ask, anyway and, by the look on Mum's face, there might never be a right time!

'You haven't told Ben and Alex about Jonathon yet, have you?' she asked, instead.

'No,' Mum said, 'but I will, I promise. I'll do it tonight but I'll be a bit late. I've got a meeting at five that'll go on for at least an hour. You got any plans today?'

'Not really. I might go out later, if anyone's around, I don't know.'

'OK, well, take care.'

Mum opened the door but she didn't go out.

'Jessie,' she said. 'I love you. You know that, don't you?'

''Course,' said Jessica.

'And your dad loves you too,' she added, quietly.

Jessica nodded. She didn't know what else to do or say. Mum looked as if she was about to say something else but she didn't. Instead she hugged Jessica, squeezing her tight before suddenly letting go and hurrying out. Jessica watched Mum walking down the path before closing the door. She shivered as she stood in the hall. The sudden mention of Dad was well strange. What was going on, why did it feel as if life was spiralling out of control again? Whatever was happening, she didn't much like it.

She walked slowly back upstairs. She wouldn't bother going out today after all. She'd have a shower, get dressed, maybe curl up and watch some crap breakfast TV to take her mind off things or finish sorting out her web pages. In an hour or so, she could maybe phone Kal. Chill out, like the boys had said – have a quiet, peaceful day.

9

'Louise!'

The sound of her name and the draught, as the bathroom door was pushed open, woke Louise. She sat up, cracking her head on the side of the loo. The pain made her close her eyes again, momentarily, and when she opened them, she saw Cate standing in the bathroom doorway, arms folded, staring at the papers from the folder, which were still scattered. Without all her make-up Cate looked younger, more like Louise than ever.

'I, er,' said Louise, rubbing her head.

'Don't tell me,' said Cate, 'you like sleeping on bathroom floors, so much more comfortable than a bed!'

The sarcasm was slightly better than the anger Louise had feared.

'I was sick,' said Louise, 'then I must have fallen asleep.'

'Oh well,' said Cate, looking at the floor, 'at least you didn't throw up over my stuff. Although I'm not sure what you were doing nicking it in the first place.'

'I didn't steal it,' Louise snapped, shuffling forward, collecting some of the papers together. 'I just wanted to look at it and why shouldn't I?'

Her head hurt, her stomach felt strained, her throat was sore, her mouth was all furry and disgusting and she really couldn't be doing with Cate right now.

'It's all right,' said Cate smirking down at her, 'no need to get in a strop. I half expected you to look but the other half didn't think you'd have the guts.'

'Well I have,' said Louise, shoving some of the papers back in the folder, 'and I did!'

'And?' said Cate.

'You don't really believe this stuff?' said Louise, gathering the sheets highlighted in orange.

She got up and sat on the edge of the bath, the highlighted papers in her hand, waving them at Cate.

'What's not to believe?' said Cate. 'It's fact, Louise, not fiction. It's hardly news, is it? It started way back in the nineteenth century, can you believe that?'

'No,' said Louise, looking through the papers, 'but that's what it says here.'

'Took them a while to get the hang of it,' said Cate. 'They couldn't get going seriously until the technology caught up with the ideas – like Leonardo da Vinci and his helicopters. Anyway, the first really big break didn't come till 1996.'

'Dolly?' said Louise, the name making her shiver.

'Yep,' said Cate, 'Dolly, probably the most famous sheep in history. All a bit hit-and-miss, in those days, but they've been getting better all the time. The Japanese had a success rate of seven out of a thousand with those frozen mice but now – well you've read the stats. The technique's pretty bloody perfect. Live tissue, frozen tissue, rats, pigs, monkeys, someone's pet cat, woolly mammoths, you name it, they can clone it. OK, so they haven't quite got it right with the mammoths yet, but give them time.'

The C word seemed to fill the bathroom, Louise could almost see it scrawled on the white-tiled walls, hear it echoing: CLONE.

'But that's animals, not people!' she said. 'No one's done it with people, unless you believe any of those loopy religious groups.'

'I don't and I never said they had.'

'But that's what you think. You think . . .'

'You a mind-reader now or what?' said Cate.

'No! But this stuff about Jessica's granddad, or adoptive granddad, being a scientist! Why didn't you tell me?'

'I was going to,' said Cate. 'I was gonna pick my time that's all. I didn't want you flipping out on me, fainting, throwing up – like you do.'

'Can you blame me?' said Louise standing up. 'He worked on cloning! He's done it with animals and you think he did it with us!'

'Facts, Louise, let's stick to facts,' said Cate, her voice sounding vacant, far away, somehow. 'He worked on cloning, then just after that second mammoth project that almost worked, he quit, retired, whatever, and some years later died of an overdose – accidental, allegedly.'

'But you think it's connected,' Louise insisted. 'You think that sometime before he retired, he took a break from mammoths and started on humans.'

'Humans would be way easier than mammoths, I reckon,' said Cate.

'I don't care,' Louise heard herself shouting. 'He didn't do it, he couldn't, it's illegal, it's not allowed. They couldn't do that. There's a whole set of rules, laws. You've got most of them printed out in your bloody folder. I'm not a clone. I'm not a bloody freak!'

Cate laughed.

'Sorry,' she said, 'I know it's not funny. It's just the way you swear in that posh voice of yours.'

Louise dropped the papers she'd been holding and sat down again, clutching the edges of the bath, trying to stop tears spilling out but it was too late. Cate calmly picked up the papers and folder, putting everything back together.

'That's why I don't tell you everything,' Cate announced, walking over towards the loo. 'You just get all hysterical on me.'

'Like I said, can you blame me?' said Louise, sniffing and wiping the tears with a bit of loo roll Cate had handed her.

Louise got up and walked over to the sink to clean her teeth, desperate to get the sharp, acidic taste out of her mouth.

'Well, it doesn't exactly help, does it?' Cate was saying. 'I mean look at the state of you! It's probably all bollocks anyway. It was just another theory I was looking at, that's all,' she added, though she didn't sound very convincing.

Louise finished brushing her teeth and splashed her face with cold water.

'I don't suppose you've got a picture of Jessica's granddad, have you?' she asked, as she patted her face dry on an incredibly soft, white towel.

'No, but I could easily find one. Why?'

'It probably wouldn't help,' said Louise, bile churning and churning, rising up, filling her mouth with the acidic taste again. 'I can't really remember what he looked like but there used to be an older guy with Dr Jay. Did you ever see him?'

'I don't think so,' said Cate. 'I don't remember anyone. I mean, I wasn't seriously going down that route. I still think it's all connected with fertility treatment not least because I haven't been able to track down any connection between Jessica's granddad and Dr Jay. But if what you say is right and you saw him with her. Then there's . . .'

'What?'

Louise turned to look at Cate. Was it her imagination or was Cate looking a bit pale, more stressed, less in control than usual?

'Last night,' Cate said hesitantly, as if she was having trouble forming the words or choosing the right ones, 'I remembered something. I tried to check it out on line. I didn't find what I was after but I've got a horrible feeling . . . I still can't quite see the connections though!'

'Well tell me, let me help!'

Before Cate could respond, a tune suddenly trilled out from Louise's com, which was still lying on the floor, where she'd left it. Cate clutched her folder in one hand, picked up the com with the other and handed it to Louise.

'It's my mother,' Louise said.

'Well answer it then!'

Louise managed to mutter 'hi' when there was a knock on the bedroom door.

'Iain,' Cate mouthed.

Louise followed Cate into the bedroom, talking to her mother as she walked, trying to make her voice sound steady, normal, hoping her mother couldn't hear the loud, unnatural thump of her heart.

'No, I'm fine, a bit tired that's all. I don't know. I thought I might stay on at Naomi's for a while, if that's all right? What? Dr Jay? She phoned you? Why, what did she want?'

Louise waved at Cate and Iain, signalling them over. Cate signalled back, indicating for Louise to turn up the volume on the com.

'I don't quite know,' Louise's mother said. 'She was asking whether you were all right, which seemed a bit strange, as she'd only seen you a couple of days ago.'

A couple of days that seemed like an entire life-time ago!

'I told her you were staying with a friend and she asked me which friend and whether I was sure. I mean, you are with Naomi, aren't you, darling? Louise, are you still there?' she added after a slight pause. 'Are you sure you're all right?'

Louise tried to speak but her mind was still busy processing information and her mouth wouldn't work. Cate moved near to Louise and spoke into the com.

'Of course I'm with Naomi and I'm fine, Mummy,' she said in a near-perfect imitation of Louise's voice. 'I'll see you later. 'Bye!'

''Bye, darling, take care.'

'God you are *so* useless,' said Cate although she smiled as she spoke.

'But it was Dr Jay,' Louise said. 'Dr Jay phoned Mummy early this morning.'

'So I gather,' said Cate, sitting on the edge of the bed, the purple folder resting on her knees. 'Which means she's probably been in touch with Tess and Carla too.'

'But what if my parents get suspicious?' Louise said. 'What if they check with Naomi's parents, what if they've given Naomi's number to Dr Jay?'

'Why should they?' said Cate. 'Anyway, who cares, that's the least of our problems now. The fact that our Dr Jay's sniffing around means she's worried, yes?'

'Which means there's something to be worried about,' said Louise, quietly.

Cate looked down at the folder then back at Louise.

'Yeah, well I think we know that,' said Cate, in a way that made Louise shiver.

'What's going on?' said Iain. 'Have I missed something again?'

'Get him up to speed, Lou,' Cate said, handing her the folder. 'I'm gonna get dressed. I won't be long. We really, really need to see Jessica.'

She started picking up her clothes. Louise noticed she picked up her phone too before going towards the bathroom, obviously up to something secretive and devious again. So who was she going to contact, was she going to phone Jessica?

'Hi, Jessica, this is one of your clones speaking. Mind if I pop round and see you!'

Clone – she couldn't get the word, the idea, out of her mind even though she knew it was totally impossible.

'Wait,' Louise said, as Cate was about to

disappear behind the bathroom door. 'Just before my mother called, you said you'd remembered something. You said you'd been looking something up.'

'Yeah,' said Cate, 'but I can't find any proof and I hope I'm wrong 'cos it's way freakier than anything we've put together so far. But you know that Katherine person Dr Jay mentioned?'

Louise nodded.

'Well,' said Cate. 'I've got a horrible feeling I know who she is.'

'Bloody typical,' Louise yelled, standing up and hurling the folder at the bathroom door, as it slammed shut behind Cate. 'As if it's not bad enough without all her bloody secrets. Why can't she just tell us? If she'd told me about Jessica and her bloody granddad from the start we might have got a whole lot further!'

'Hey,' said Iain, coming towards her, putting his arms round her, hugging her close. 'Come on, it's OK, it'll be OK.'

Louise let him hold her for a while before pulling away, not least because she knew she smelt vile. Iain didn't seem to notice though. He gently pushed loose strands of hair behind her ear before touching her forehead with his finger.

'You've got a bruise coming up,' he said. 'Cate's not been attacking you, has she?'

Louise laughed, the tension in her stomach, her muscles relaxing slightly almost for the first time since she'd set eyes on Cate.

'Only with the usual verbals,' she said. 'I banged my head on the loo.'

She edged back a little further as Iain continued to look at her. There was an attraction between them, she could sense it. Not that she had a lot of experience of this sort of thing so she could be wrong. Did Iain really like her or did he just see Cate when he looked at her? Or maybe he just felt sorry for her. Iain shook his head slightly, as if he might be wondering much the same sort of thing, then he went over and picked up the folder, which had mercifully been fastened up when she'd hurled it at the door.

'Come on,' he said, perching on the edge of the bed. 'Come and tell me what Jessica's granddad's got to do with anything.'

Louise nodded and sat beside him. How could she be thinking of anything as normal as fancying someone with the Frankenstein folder sitting between them? For a while all Louise could hear, as she showed Iain the relevant print-outs, was the shower running, the rustle of paper and

Iain's muttered, mainly incredulous, yet somehow reassuring, comments – *this is mad, she's flipped, clones now for Christ's sake* – but soon she heard something else, the sound of Cate's raised voice coming from the bathroom.

The shower was still running but obviously Cate wasn't showering; she'd left it on to drown the sound of her phone calls but it wasn't quite working because her voice was getting ever louder.

'I mean this can't be right,' Iain was muttering. 'They'd have known, they'd have said.'

They, who was he on about? Louise was going to ask but Cate was shouting really loudly now so Louise got up and walked over to the bathroom door.

'Never mind that, now,' Cate was saying, 'just answer the question. It's simple enough, what was her name? Don't lie to me! Yeah, OK, I'll stop lying too. I know more than you think and I'm gonna find out the rest with or without your help.'

That didn't sound like a Jessica conversation. That was the tone people used when they were pissed off with their parents. It was Tess or Carla that Cate was talking to.

'Never mind why I want to know! A name, that's all I want,' Cate was saying, 'a simple bloody name! All right, I'll tell you, will that make it easier? It was Katherine, wasn't it?'

Why was Cate asking Tess or Carla about Katherine? There was silence for a moment, then Cate's voice again but it was too quiet for Louise to make out more than a couple of words. Louise edged closer so she was leaning against the door but Cate's voice had dropped to a whisper then stopped altogether. Before Louise could start to move, the bathroom door opened, almost knocking her over. Cate barely seemed to notice as she barged out, fully dressed, lightly made-up and with the phone in her hand.

'Shower's on,' she told Louise, 'so grab your clothes and be quick; we're going to Jessica's. Iain, get your stuff and pay the bill, we'll meet you at the car.'

'OK,' said Iain, ever obedient to Cate's whims, 'tell me Jessica's address and I'll set the Sat-Nav.'

'Hang on,' said Louise, as Cate scribbled the address for Iain before snatching clothes from the top of Louise's bag and shoving them at her.

'The good news,' said Cate, 'is that Jessica's expecting us.'

'How, I mean what did she say, what did you tell her?' Iain asked.

'And the bad news?' Louise said, more or less at the same time.

'There's quite a lot of bad news,' said Cate, 'but I'm not sure quite how bad. I'll tell you in the car,' Cate said, virtually pushing her into the bathroom. 'And yes, I promise. I'll tell you everything. You're really not gonna like it but I'll tell you anyway.'

Jessica stood in the hall with a towel wrapped round her, staring at the house phone, wondering if she'd imagined the call or what. She sat down on the bottom stair and was still looking at the phone when she heard her com. She raced back upstairs and picked it up off her bed, hardly daring to look, but it was only Kaleem.

'Hi,' she said, 'I'm glad it's you! I've just had this crank call on the house phone. I thought for a minute they'd got my com number as well.'

'What kind of crank call?'

'Some woman with a Scottish accent – might have been fake. God knows how these people find the numbers.'

'What people, what you on about? It was probably just someone wanting to sell you life insurance.'

'No – she said she wanted to talk about my granddad.'

'The one we were talking about last night?'

'Yeah – seemed a bit weird, bit of a coincidence.'

'So who was it?'

'I don't know. I don't even know how she got our number. She said she was called Cate. Cate with a C – as if I'm supposed to care how she spells her bloody name!'

'So what did she want to talk about exactly?'

'I don't know. She didn't say much. She was like all sort of secretive – whispering like someone might be listening in. And when I tried to call back it was just a messaging service.'

'Bit weird,' Kal said.

Jessica sat down on the edge of the bed.

'Tell me about it!' she said. 'It's like living some freaky novel – you know – with Dr Jay turning up last night and now this nutter wanting to talk about Granddad.'

'Yeah well if someone starts trying to hack the door down with a machete, you let me know all right?'

Jessica laughed, changed the subject and talked about Kal's brother's impending wedding for a while. She felt fine when she was talking to Kal but as soon as the call ended her mind flashed back to the other call. She hadn't told Kal everything;

she hadn't told him the main bit about the mystery caller threatening to turn up! She hadn't wanted to worry him 'cos there was absolutely nothing he could do stuck up there in Manchester. Besides she wouldn't need any help, she'd be fine. She'd just do what she was always wanting characters in books to do – don't play the hero, think and be sensible!

She could phone Mum although there wasn't much point. She could hardly ask Mum to come home on the off chance that some hoax caller was actually going to turn up. She could maybe ask if she knew anyone called Kate though or 'Cate with a C'! The woman – or maybe girl 'cos she'd sounded quite young – had asked for Mum at first but sounded relieved when she'd said she was at work.

Cate with a C was probably one of those loony protestor types, an animal rights activist. Although why she'd be going on about Granddad, a scientist who'd been dead nearly ten years, Jessica couldn't quite imagine. Any serious protestor would surely be too busy campaigning outside that new lab they'd opened in Surrey but then you could never tell what went on in their heads. It wasn't like you were talking sane or normal here; these people were complete nutters who thought animals should have the same rights as people.

She stood up and opened her wardrobe, trying not to think about protestors but they just made her so mad! If it was left to them there'd be no medicines, no animal-human organ transplants, no inoculations and the last flu outbreak would have gone totally pandemic. This was the 'let's put cute little piggies before humans' brigade! Let's burn down the labs and plant bombs under scientists' cars. Very humane, very sensible!

She grabbed at her towel as it started to slip. Right, focus, think! First thing she needed to do was get dressed. She'd been in the shower when the phone rang and hadn't even had a chance to get properly dry. She pulled some jeans out of the wardrobe, trying to remember what loopy Cate with a C had said. She hadn't said much but it had been so weird, so unexpected and she'd spoken so fast it was hard to take anything in. *This is important. But you need to prepare yourself for a bit of a shock,* that's what she'd said.

Well, no way! She'd had enough shocks for one week with Mum and Jonathon's engagement and Dr Jay turning up, without waiting for some lunatic to lob a brick through their window. She wriggled into her jeans and grabbed her favourite top. She'd go out, get out of the house. Dan, she was fairly sure, had another day off and Emma's parents were so rich she didn't need to work so at least one of those two would be around. Then she could mention the freaky phone call to Mum tonight. Sorted! And if there were any more calls, if the woman kept hassling her, if she came back to find the house wrecked, they could contact the police. Hopefully though it wouldn't come to that.

She put her top on, looked in the mirror, added a pair of earrings to the outfit but decided she couldn't be bothered with make-up, then picked up her bag and was about to go downstairs when the doorbell rang. She stopped at the top of the stairs. Ignore it, don't answer it. No, that was stupid. She moved down two steps. It wouldn't be the Cate person. About an hour, she'd said; if she was going to turn up at all, if it wasn't a hoax. It was more likely the postman, bringing the books she'd ordered. She moved down another step then stopped as the doorbell rang again, longer this time. OK let it ring. If it was the postman he could leave the parcel outside or with a neighbour. On the other hand she could stop being so flaming pathetic and answer the door.

As she moved towards the bottom of the stairs, two envelopes, one white, one brown slid through the flap. So it *was* the postman! She darted forward, slipped, scrambled up and opened the door just as he reached the gate. He turned back and handed her the parcel, scowling as if she'd caused him a lot of trouble. She took the parcel inside. She wanted to open it, curl up with a drink and the next Sol adventure but no, she was dressed now, she'd stick to Plan A and take herself off away from any possible trouble.

She dumped the parcel on the kitchen table and headed back to the hall, checking in her bag as she went, like Mum always did. Satisfied that she'd got everything, she opened the door to see someone standing right there in front of her on the doorstep. She thought for a minute it was the postman who'd come back but it looked nothing like the postman.

'Oh, shit!' Jessica said.

10

Despite her total exhaustion, the ever-present sickness and the C word that she just couldn't get out of her mind, Louise showered and dressed quicker than she'd ever managed. She could hear the word Clone in the gush of the water, imagined it printed on the front of her T-shirt; could almost feel it wrapping itself round her like it was going to haunt her for the rest of her life. She shook her head as she left the bathroom, trying to shake the word away.

Cate's bag was by the door and she was just shutting down her micro. What had she been checking out this time, what was left to check? Louise's hair was still wet so she quickly gathered it into a high ponytail, twisted it round, fastened it and hid the whole lot under a hat.

'Bit better than your old prep school boater,' said Cate, 'but not a lot. Hurry up,' Cate added, barely giving Louise time to fasten up her bag. 'Iain's paid and brought the car round.'

Cate seemed to be back to her bossy, confident self, as if the conversation about clones had never happened, as if she didn't care that they might have been manufactured from some spare tissue, some random strands of DNA. She rushed out leaving Louise to follow, wondering whether Cate's earlier cryptic comment about Katherine was going to be another exercise in evasion but when they got to the car Cate got in the back with her, clearly ready to talk.

'Shouldn't take long to Jessica's,' Cate said, 'or at least it shouldn't once we get going,' she added, pointedly, leaning towards the driver's seat. 'Iain, it might help if you actually set off.'

'Oh, right, yes,' said Iain, who'd been looking out of the wing mirrors, apparently happily watching cars going in and out of the car park.

'Turn right,' the Nav system said in a soft Scottish accent when they eventually began to move.

'Left, you idiot,' Iain muttered, 'we're still in the car park and it's one way.'

'Just drive,' Cate said, 'and listen – but maybe not too hard or you'll be crashing the car. OK,' she said, turning to Louise, 'the first bit of bad news is that I phoned the café this morning but neither Tess nor Carla was there.'

'But I thought I heard you talking to them.'

'I did – eventually,' said Cate. 'But they weren't at the café, which was weird 'cos they never take a day off when the café's busy, certainly not both of them together. And Mavis didn't seem to know where they were – just that they'd said they wouldn't be in. Iain, what the hell are you doing? The exit's that way – we've been round the bloody car park twice already.'

'Yes, sorry,' he muttered.

'So what are you saying? What do you think's going on with Tess and Carla?' Louise asked, as Iain finally headed for the exit.

'I'm not sure,' said Cate. 'Anyway – so then I called Tess's mobile. She's a bit easier to bully than Carla but she wasn't keen to tell me much. Not least 'cos she was too busy fretting about me, asking a whole load of stupid questions.'

It was hardly surprising they were fretting! Louise could barely imagine how her own parents would react if she took off for a week with a boyfriend or if they knew what she was doing, who she was with, right now, but then, from what she'd heard, Tess and Carla were a touch more laid-back than her parents.

'It was like we were edging round each other all the time,' Cate was saying. 'I wouldn't say where I was and Tess wouldn't tell me what they were doing.'

'I heard you asking about Katherine,' Louise said. 'Tess and Carla know someone called Katherine, right?'

'Mmm,' said Cate, as if she wasn't sure.

'But it's a pretty common name.'

'Turn left.'

'Will you turn that bloody Sat-Nav down,' Cate said.

She bit her bottom lip and did that weird narrowing thing with her eyes before she spoke again.

'OK – back to Katherine. Yes, it's a common enough name but I think being with you is starting to get to me, Lou, because I've been straying into seriously spooky territory with Katherine.'

'Meaning?'

'OK, bear with me on this one for a bit.'

Louise sighed. Nothing, but nothing was ever straightforward with Cate!

'You know how people have heart transplants and stuff?' Cate began.

'Transplants!' Louise almost screamed. 'You

181

think we've all been cloned for spare parts for this Katherine person?'

She heard a sharp intake of breath from Iain followed by a short, harsh laugh from Cate.

'No, you dozo,' Cate said. 'I know this is all a bit weird, to say the least, but it's not that bloody weird – I hope. Nobody's gonna be nicking any of my bits, no way, not for anyone! Besides if they wanted to do something like that they'd just grow the parts not a whole person.'

She said the last part almost casually; in that way she had of making the most bizarre conversations seem perfectly logical, perfectly reasonable. How on earth did Cate manage to stay so – detached?

'No,' she went on, 'what I mean is have you heard of any of these cases where people claim their personality's changed after a transplant?'

'Well, yes,' said Louise, 'there was a woman who started reading Dickens and stuff after a heart transplant, when she'd barely opened a book in her life before.'

'And it's not just hearts,' said Cate. 'One guy took up classical guitar after a kidney transplant. He'd never been musical but he just suddenly taught himself to play.'

'And the point is?' came Iain's voice from the front.

'Residual memories,' said Cate, 'some people think the brain's not the only organ to store memories. So when someone has a transplant they can take on some of the personality, some of the memory, of the donor.'

'That's bollocks,' said Iain. 'Isn't it?'

'No, it's science,' said Cate. 'There've been so many cases that doctors are researching it pretty seriously now.'

Was this the sort of information Cate carried around in her head or had she been looking it up? Was that what she'd been doing with her micro? Cate certainly hadn't suffered by not going to school – she seemed to know tons about absolutely everything!

'And anyway,' Iain was saying, 'what's it got to do with you or Louise or this Katherine? No one's had a transplant, have they?'

'Not exactly,' said Cate, answering Iain though keeping her eyes firmly fixed on Louise. 'But remember when you told me about your freaky dream and I said my mums had a friend who was stabbed to death like that?'

Louise nodded, as her chest started to tighten.

As usual, she didn't quite know where Cate was leading but she was starting to get a fair idea and felt pretty sure she wasn't going to like it.

'Well, I remembered something else,' said Cate, 'or at least I thought I did.'

Louise could picture the moment when it had happened; after she'd explained the dream, when Cate had seemed to be searching for something deep in her mind and not really liked what she'd found.

'I remembered,' Cate said, 'that she was called Kathy. I remembered Carla had called her Kathy. Kathy – Katherine?'

A picture appeared in front of Louise's eyes, like a still from a film. Only this was a frame from her dream, the extended version of the dream where she looked down at the body, the person who was her, yet not quite her; lying on the path, clothes slashed, blood everywhere. Katherine, oh God, could that have been Katherine, is that what Cate was getting at?

'And were you right?' Louise asked, barely able to force the words out. 'What did Tess say?'

'She got in a complete flap, which I took as a yes. I think we can safely say that their friend who was stabbed was called Katherine and that it's got something to do with us.'

'Hang on,' said Iain, as Louise started to retch and opened the window just in case. 'You're serious about this cloning business, aren't you? You're saying that Louise's nightmare might be a memory, Katherine's memory?'

A memory, could he be right? Not a premonition but something that had already happened – a real murder of a real person, a person who'd been somehow resurrected through them. If people picked up memories from a transplanted kidney, or a heart, how many would you have if you were cloned?

'You really believe you were cloned?' Iain was saying. 'You think you were cloned from this dead person, this Katherine, and that Tess and Carla knew about it! No, no way, that's crazy!'

'Is it?' said Cate. 'Well, good, that's great, because right now I'd be quite happy to believe I was just going mad.'

Cate was right; Great-Aunt Mary-style paranoia and madness were starting to look like really attractive options because if they weren't mad, if they weren't jumping to completely bizarre conclusions . . . Louise shook her head. She could barely begin to cope with the implications. Her brain wouldn't go there, not fully, not totally. No way could it be true. She couldn't begin to know what Tess and Carla might sanction but no way would her parents agree to anything like that. And why should they, what possible connection could they have to Katherine?

'Iain's right,' said Louise, looking directly at Cate, 'it's not possible, it doesn't make sense. Why her, why clone this murdered Katherine? And anyway if it was true, what you're saying, we'd both have the memories, the dreams, wouldn't we?'

'You'd think so,' said Cate, 'but it's probably not that straightforward. Brains are funny things, sort of complex.'

'I know that,' said Louise, 'I have actually got a brain, you know, I'm not thick.'

'What I mean,' said Cate, 'is that we might have the same basic brain but it's got wired up differently. Or maybe I do have the dreams and just don't remember them. I told you I never really remember dreams very well but I do wake up disorientated, like I said. As if I've been somewhere far away, somewhere weird, somewhere that's not really part of my life. So who knows? I could have the same dream as you but just not remember. Different wiring, see?'

Cate was doing it again, sounding casual,

detached, talking about wiring like she was discussing plugs not their brains! It was like she wasn't taking any of this seriously at all, as if it was all happening to someone else, not them.

'And we'd be more alike, wouldn't we,' Louise pressed on, 'in personality? We'd both be like her, like Katherine. We'd have more Katherine memories, all the time. We wouldn't be us, we'd be her!'

The thought made her retch again and she leant towards the window. How could she not be Louise, how could she be someone else with someone else's thoughts and memories?

'I don't think so,' said Cate. 'I've just told you, it's all about wiring, the way your brain links up all its little neurological pathways when you're growing up. We've been brought up different, haven't we? I mean like you talk posh and I don't. Different experiences, different results – it's not all about genes. And anyway we won't know how much like Katherine we are till we find out about her.'

Oh great, now Cate was talking about it as though it was all fixed, all proved and she was still totally calm!

'I can't believe you're even talking about this,' said Iain. 'And I think we're nearly there by the way.'

Louise leant out of the open window, taking in gulps of air. Sometime while they'd been talking, they'd left the motorway and were now on some wide tree-lined road.

'At the roundabout turn right,' the Sat-Nav said, as Iain turned it up slightly.

'So what are we going to do when we get there?' Louise asked.

'I was gonna try and be a bit subtle,' Cate said, 'try to break it to Jessica gently. But maybe direct is best. Get it over with quick, eh? Besides, maybe Jessica already knows.'

Jessica stirred the coffee before putting the milk back in the fridge. She couldn't believe she was doing this. She couldn't believe she'd even let her in but then she hadn't had much choice.

'Is your mother in?' Dr Jay had said, as she stood on the doorstep.

'Er, no, she's at work.'

'Good,' Dr Jay had said, pushing the door open a bit wider and walking in before Jessica could stop her, 'because it's you I want to talk to.'

The offer of a drink hadn't been made out of politeness. It was to stall for time, to allow her a minute or so alone in the kitchen. She picked up the two mugs and turned to see Dr Jay standing in the kitchen doorway. How long had Dr Jay been there, what had she seen? Jessica was going to take the coffee through to the lounge but Dr Jay had already walked into the kitchen and perched on one of the stools at the breakfast bar. Jessica put one of the mugs down in front of her and went to stand over by the sink.

'Thank you,' Dr Jay said. 'I hope you don't mind me coming round but I needed to talk to you on your own.'

'Was it you?' Jessica asked, as a thought struck her. 'Did you phone earlier?'

'Phone, no, why, have you had a strange call?'

'No,' Jessica said, 'no, it's nothing. Cold call, I expect.'

She wasn't sure she believed Dr Jay. It seemed the sort of thing Dr Jay might do, somehow: put on a silly Scottish accent, check that Mum was out. She waited for Dr Jay to speak, to explain why she was here but she didn't. She just sipped her coffee and stared in that intense way. She'd clearly come back for a reason so wait it out. All she had to do was be patient, wait for Dr Jay to tell her what it was. Oh God, maybe she was about to announce that she and Dad were getting married or were married already!

'So what do you want to talk to me about?' Jessica said, unnerved by the stare, unable to wait any longer.

'I think it's time,' said Dr Jay slowly, 'that we – that I – explained a few things.'

'About Dad,' Jessica said.

'In a way, yes.'

'Well you don't need to bother,' said Jessica, 'I already know!'

Her announcement got the sort of reaction she'd been expecting.

'You know,' said Dr Jay, her face turning pale beneath her make-up. 'How?'

'Mum told me last night, after you left.'

'Your mother told you?'

Jessica frowned, wishing Dr Jay would get on with what she wanted to say instead of repeating everything like some sort of neurotic parrot.

'Not outright,' Jessica said, 'but I guessed. It wasn't hard.'

Dr Jay's face relaxed slightly, the colour started to return.

'What did you guess, Jessica?' she asked, her voice cold but with a hint of mockery.

'Don't treat me like an idiot,' said Jessica. 'I know about you and Dad. I know about the affair and I think Granddad knew too. I think that's why he had the row with Dad. I think that's why he died.'

Jessica stopped abruptly, not quite sure why she'd said all that. It wasn't what she really believed but it seemed as if she might have been right. Dr Jay blinked at the mention of Granddad, almost as if she was going to cry though she hardly seemed the crying type, somehow. She stood up, walked a couple of paces further away from Jessica then turned.

'I can see why your mother might have let you believe that, Jessica,' she said, 'but it isn't true. I didn't have an affair with your father.'

She laughed slightly as she spoke, like she was enjoying some sick, private joke.

'Yeah, right!'

'I can't make you believe me,' she said, 'but I don't think your dad would have had an affair with anyone and certainly not with me.'

'Meaning?'

'Meaning we weren't exactly the best of friends, especially after – well, I was never entirely honest with your parents, Jessica, I wasn't honest with anyone, and I regret that now, in a way, but it was all so difficult. We had to be so careful.'

Never entirely honest – it was like Dr Jay was deliberately talking in riddles, expecting Jessica to work it out for herself. Well, all right, she would. Her brain was already buzzing with possibilities. It was something Dr Jay knew. Something that she'd kept secret from Mum and Dad, something to do with Granddad's death, possibly. But then there was no real reason to discuss that with her. That was more of a whole family thing, something to discuss with Ben, Alex, Mum, Dad or all of them together. So more likely it was something more personal to her, something about her past.

'Is this something to do with my birth parents?' said Jessica, pleased with her deductions. 'Were you around that night when Granddad found me?'

'Er, no,' said Dr Jay.

OK – stupid idea. There was no one else around that night. Granddad was on his way to see Mum and Dad. He was alone. The weather was bad, there'd been heavy flooding. He was late so as soon as he'd had a chance he'd stopped to phone them, to tell them he was all right. And that's when he'd seen the carrycot in the bus shelter. As though someone had caught the late night bus and forgotten to take their baby with them; a baby that Social

Services had later been persuaded to let Mum and Dad adopt. If it was true, if any of it was true.

Thoughts were whirling around in her head like clothes in a tumble drier; all mixed up, half-crazy thoughts. *I didn't have an affair with your father,* Dr Jay had said but she'd sort of stressed *'your father'* as if she was hinting that she might have had a relationship with someone else, someone else Jessica knew. An idea flashed to the front of her mind. She dismissed it because of the age gap. There must have been at least twenty years between Dr Jay and Granddad. But the idea wouldn't quite go away. It forced its way back, refusing to be ignored.

'Was it Granddad?' Jessica said. 'Did you and Granddad – I mean am I your . . .'

'Good heavens, no!' said Dr Jay, almost shuddering. 'It was nothing like that. I've never had any children. I – well, I was a great admirer of your grandfather's work. He was a wonderful man. And yes, we were – close – for a while.'

She was doing it again. Talking in that vague, evasive, totally irritating way but stressing certain words, dropping clues. Close, she'd stressed the word close, not quite admitting anything but the implication was there. But that wasn't what she'd come to talk about. Whatever she'd had going on with Granddad couldn't matter to anyone now.

'Look, I'm sorry,' Dr Jay said, talking rapidly as she headed towards the kitchen door. 'This was a mistake. It won't work. I have to go. I should never have come. You need to talk to your mother. She can tell you, she can tell you everything – well most things.'

'Fine,' said Jessica, reaching the kitchen door before Dr Jay got there, standing in front of it, barring her way, 'but we'll both talk to her. She'll be here any minute. I phoned her when I was making the coffee.'

No way was she letting Dr Jay walk out now. She was going to find out what this was all about, tackle her and Mum together. One of them was sure to crack.

'Ah!' said Dr Jay. 'I should have known you would.'

Jessica half expected Dr Jay to try to push past her, try to leave, but she didn't. She went and sat at the breakfast bar again, rubbing her chin with her finger as if deep in thought.

'All right,' she said eventually. 'What exactly do you know about your grandfather's work, Jessica?'

11

Louise tried to empty her mind, force away the thoughts that were making her feel so ill, focus on her breathing and the bewildering geography of Milton Keynes. How did people ever manage to find their way round places like this before Sat-Nav? All the roundabouts, all the streets, all the houses looked incredibly similar. As they approached yet another roundabout Cate, who'd been leaning slightly towards her, suddenly swung her head round to look out of the back window and let out a sharp squeal that almost burst Louise's eardrums.

'That's Tess's car,' she yelped.

'What, where, are you sure?' Louise asked. 'It can't be.'

Maybe things were getting to Cate after all and she'd started imagining stuff.

'It was behind us, at the roundabout,' Cate said.

'I think it turned off left. Iain, did you see it? I'm sure it was hers.'

'Er, no, I . . .'

'Turn round, go back to the roundabout,' Cate said. 'No don't. It's there again, that red semi-electric, two cars back.'

'At the next junction,' the Sat-Nav said, 'turn left.'

'Don't turn, just slow down,' Cate shouted at Iain but she was too late.

'This is it, this is Jessica's street,' Iain said as they turned into a quiet cul-de-sac.

Even though it was the school holidays, Louise noticed that there was no one around; no kids out playing and only a couple of cars parked. The street looked much like others they'd passed. The houses were all detached, smaller and much more modern than hers with colourful gardens, hanging baskets, domed solar-pods and neatly trimmed hedges.

'I don't care,' said Cate. 'Stop and turn round.'

Iain pulled in about halfway along on the left but there was no need to turn round because the red car had followed them into the street and was pulling up a little way behind them. Louise had been sure Cate had been mistaken but clearly she hadn't been.

'It's them, it's definitely them,' Cate said, as she and Louise stared out of the rear window, watching two women get out of the red car. 'What the hell's going on? What are they doing here, how could they know? They must have been to the cops, tracked my calls. Bloody hell, that's all we need!'

Cate unclipped her seat belt and darted out of the car.

'Ah,' said Iain, as Louise prepared to follow, 'it wasn't supposed to happen quite like this. They were supposed to catch up with us before we left the services, talk things through quietly. I think you'd better wait here. This could get a bit fiery.'

But Louise was barely listening, barely taking in what Iain was saying, let alone trying to interpret it. She'd got out and was heading towards Cate, who'd met up with Tess and Carla in the middle of the street in a mass of arm waving and shouting that made it seem as though there were far more than three people involved.

The shouting and arm waving stopped as Louise approached. The two women stared at Louise then looked back towards Cate. The slightly taller, slightly slimmer, blonde woman, who Louise guessed was Tess, from a blurry photo Cate had shown her on her phone during the drive down from Harrogate, shook her head.

'O-mi-god,' the dark-haired one in the long cotton skirt and blue jacket said, looking at Louise again then towards Iain's car. 'It's true. He was right.'

'He?' said Cate, swinging round to face Iain who'd locked the car and was striding towards them. 'It was you! You told them? You phoned Tess and Carla. You told them where I was. Of all the stupid, pathetic, double-crossing – why, why did you do it?'

'Because it's his job,' Carla said, 'because we paid him to keep us informed.'

'What?' Cate snapped.

Iain shrugged, his lips twisting into an uneasy smile, an embarrassed smile that Louise felt was aimed more at her than at Cate.

'Iain's not quite what you think,' Carla said. 'He's not a student, he's a fair bit older than he looks and he works for his uncle.'

'As a private detective,' Tess added. 'I'm sorry, Cate, I'm really sorry but . . .'

A laugh escaped from Louise before she could stop it. Iain, who Cate thought she'd been so cleverly manipulating, was a private detective, hired by Tess and Carla! It was just all so bizarre, so crazy, even by the mega-weird standards of the last couple of days. Cate glared at her, forcing Louise to turn the laugh into a poorly disguised cough.

'You bastard,' Cate snarled at Iain, her face flushed and contorted. 'How could you, how could you do that? All that crap about Tess and Carla being worried, all the lies – you must have been telling them every friggin' move I've made!'

He'd certainly played his part well. Louise had thought his relationship with Cate was a bit odd but never in a million years would she have guessed that quiet, ever-so-slightly-dopey Iain was a private detective of all things. Her mind flashed back to his antics in the service station car park; he must have phoned them last night, he was expecting to see Tess and Carla who must have set off from Edinburgh in the middle of the flaming night!

She tried searching further back, trying to look for any tell-tale signs, any clues she should have picked up, but she didn't get far because Tess had started to speak. All Louise could remember was the way Iain acted differently when Cate wasn't around and his cryptic comment in the motorway café, that Cate's arrival had interrupted.

Cate thinks everyone's pretty dumb compared to her but maybe . . .

'I'm sorry,' Tess was saying, again, stretching her arms out, as if to hug Cate but Cate stepped away, refusing to look at either of her parents. 'We were so worried about you. We were sure you were onto something but we didn't know how much you'd found out. We thought about telling you ourselves.'

'Oh yeah sure, well you've only had sixteen years!'

'We didn't want you getting hurt,' Carla said. 'What was the point of telling you, messing up your life, unless we absolutely had to?'

'So we hired Iain just to get to know you at first,' Tess said, 'to try to talk to you, get you to open up.'

Tess paused, maybe waiting for a response from Cate but when it didn't happen she carried on.

'Then when you asked Iain to drive you to Harrogate – well, we knew we'd never be able to stop you if you were determined so we let Iain go along with it.'

'We thought he could keep an eye on you, keep you safe, at least,' said Carla, 'and let us know what you found out – although we never guessed, never imagined . . .'

'You could have asked me,' Cate interrupted.

'We did,' said Carla, 'but you weren't exactly forthcoming, were you? That's why we needed Iain. We thought with someone nearer your own age, you might . . .'

'Me? You're accusing me of being secretive!' said Cate. 'Oh that's just great that is! What about you and all your bloody lies? Why didn't you save me the trouble, save yourselves the trouble of paying bloody detectives? Why didn't you tell me? Why didn't you tell me about her and Jessica?'

Cate had swung round, pointing at Louise as she said the word 'her'.

'We didn't know,' said Tess, 'we didn't know about Louise or Jessica until Iain told us and even then we could barely believe it. We had to see for ourselves but I never thought, never imagined; I still can't quite believe it.'

'Yeah, right,' said Cate.

'It's true,' said Carla. 'We didn't know, I swear it. You've found out more than we ever knew. They didn't tell us! We thought it was just you.'

Louise watched Tess and Carla as they spoke. They looked and sounded genuine enough, almost as confused as she still was but Cate looked doubtful. Her eyes had narrowed dangerously and her forehead had screwed into a frown.

'Just me?' said Cate. 'But you knew I was cloned, you knew about that? It's true, isn't it, I'm right, aren't I?'

Louise held her breath, waiting for Tess or Carla to deny it, to tell Cate she was being stupid, to offer some other explanation. Iain looked as if he was waiting for them to deny it too but they didn't. Instead Carla looked at Tess who gave a slight, almost imperceptible, nod.

'Katherine?' said Cate, her voice hard, bitter. 'We're cloned from your friend, Katherine, from some bloody dead woman, aren't we?'

This time there was no nod but it was clear from the way the colour vanished from Carla's face and from Tess's quiet tears that Cate was right. And it was clear from Iain's face that he hadn't known the full story. Whatever Tess and Carla had told him he was supposed to be investigating, it obviously wasn't the truth.

'Jesus,' said Iain, the final syllable turning into a low whistle, a whistle that seemed to hang in the air, freeze time for a moment, as Louise tried to take it in.

This wasn't, Louise knew, a mad theory any

more, it wasn't Cate playing freaky mind games, it wasn't imagination, or a bizarre hoax – it was real. Real yet impossible to believe, to even begin to understand. What would happen now? It was sure to get out, people would find out, the press, the media, her friends, the whole bloody world would know soon.

The scream, Cate's scream, unfroze the tableau. Cate had lurched towards Carla, as if she was going to hit her but Iain grabbed her, held her back, as Cate kicked at his shins and tried to bite his arm.

Tess started to cry, while Carla was talking at Cate trying to calm her, making it worse as Cate writhed and screamed, eventually forcing Iain to let her go. Cate who'd constantly mocked Louise's hysterics had lost it completely, shouting and swearing in between the screaming and stamping, her arms waving, lashing out everywhere. Louise stepped back as the whirlwind arms flailed in her direction. It was as though Cate had been bottling everything up, just waiting for final confirmation before she exploded, while Louise could now barely feel anything any more. She stood on the pavement, well away from Cate, feeling as if a huge black hole had suddenly opened up in her brain, Katherine's brain, sucking in all her emotions, the nausea, the tangle of thoughts, everything, so all she was left with was empty numbness.

Louise turned from them all, wanting to get away, to be on her own, to go somewhere; anywhere but here. She didn't move though partly because she couldn't make her limbs work properly any more and partly because a woman in a grey trouser suit and pale pink shirt had just turned into the cul-de-sac and was heading, purposefully, towards them. Had the others noticed or were they too busy shouting at each other? The woman paused for a second taking in the noise, the chaos, then she hurried on directly towards Louise.

Jessica glanced at the kitchen clock. Mum was taking her time and the conversation with Dr Jay was going nowhere fast. Dr Jay just kept quizzing her about science in general and Granddad's work in particular, like it was some sort of test – not just a test on the technicalities either but all the bloody ethics behind it. Jessica guessed she'd passed the test anyway. Well, she would; there really wasn't much she didn't know about Granddad's work. It was just all the personal stuff that was missing. With any luck they might be heading in that direction. Dr Jay might be able to tell her something new about how or why Granddad died, especially if they were as close as she'd hinted.

'You're very knowledgeable, Jessica,' Dr Jay was saying, 'very impressive. And you understand how important, how significant, your grandfather's work was, don't you?'

'Yeah, I've told you. He was amazing, really brilliant. But I'm guessing you didn't just come to test me on biology and genetics.'

'No, I didn't,' said Dr Jay, 'but having a scientific mind, seeing the need for progress, might help – might help you understand what I'm going to tell you. Although I'm not sure it was ever about the science at all, at least not for me.'

Dr Jay stood up, moving closer to Jessica who was still hovering by the kitchen door, guarding the escape route. Somewhere in the background Jessica could hear shouting – probably the neighbours yelling at their kids again. Not exactly unusual in the holidays, but Dr Jay didn't seem to notice the noise. She was staring in that creepy way she had, like she was trying to see right into your head. Trying to implant some thoughts without the need for anything as messy as speech!

'Oh God,' Dr Jay said, 'this is so difficult, so impossible. I really don't know where to start.'

'The beginning might be good,' Jessica said, trying to focus through all the noise. 'Just tell me what this is all about.'

'Yes, you're right,' said Dr Jay, 'the beginning, of course. The thing is, Jessica, I know how you feel about your parents splitting up because something similar happened to me.'

'Hey,' said Jessica, 'if this is some sort of bonding exercise, forget it. When I said the beginning I didn't mean your flaming life history. I just want to know about Dad and Granddad and my birth parents and whatever else you've all been hiding.'

'I know,' said Dr Jay, 'and I'll explain it all. But this is important. I was a bit older than you when it happened – twelve, almost thirteen. The affair had been going on for years, apparently, but things had changed – my father's lady friend was pregnant.'

'What the heck's going on out there?' said Jessica, as the shouting got louder, more aggressive, making it impossible to concentrate.

'I don't know,' said Dr Jay, as if she didn't much care either, 'but someone doesn't sound very happy.'

Jessica opened the kitchen door slightly. Something about the voices had caught her attention but Dr Jay ignored the growing noise and went on.

'I should have hated them,' she said, 'my

step-mother and the baby, but somehow I didn't. Helena, Dad's new wife, was fun and my new half-sister – I don't know – she was just the most perfect baby. Everyone adored her. She was so clever, so beautiful, the sort of kid who made everyone smile just by being there. She could have grown up spoilt, selfish, I guess, with all the attention she got, but she didn't. She never lost that natural love of life, that innocence almost.'

Although Jessica was taking in what Dr Jay was saying, she couldn't quite get the point, see the relevance to anything. And most of her attention was still on the shouting out on the street. She couldn't make out any words but the sounds, the accents, were distinctive; Scottish, like the woman on the phone.

'Oh shit,' said Jessica, 'this is all we need. I think it might be some sort of demonstration, animal rights loonies or something. It sounds like the nutter who phoned earlier.'

Dr Jay was clearly listening now too, looking even more tense and uncomfortable than before.

'Is this something to do with you?' Jessica said. 'Did you work on some of that controversial stuff with Granddad? Have they followed you here or what?'

'It's not protestors, as such,' said Dr Jay, her voice flat, resigned. 'I think I know who it is. I recognize the voices.'

'So are you going to tell me?' said Jessica. 'Or shall I find out for myself?'

She sort of knew the answer to that one. If she waited for Dr Jay to open up she'd be here forever. She checked that she had her mobile in case there was any trouble then headed for the door.

The woman in grey stopped when she was a few paces away from Louise.

'Jessie,' she said, 'what's going on?'

Something in the way she said the name, Jessie, told Louise who the woman was even before she took a step closer, blinked, rubbed her forehead and peered at Louise with a look of increasing horror.

'I'm not Jessica,' Louise said.

A pointless admission because the woman, who just had to be Jessica's mother, already knew, had already realized. Her gaze had wandered to Cate who'd managed to free herself from Iain and was standing, not very far away, yelling at Carla, until she suddenly became aware of the woman's presence.

Cate stopped yelling and the time-freezing,

slow-motion thing happened again with everyone looking at each other, apparently unable to speak or move. It was like looking at a cartoon with people's expressions exaggerated and static. The weird thing, the really weird thing, Louise realized, was that the woman, Jessica's mum, didn't seem shocked to see two replicas of her daughter. Anxious, definitely, angry maybe, confused, scared even, but not exactly surprised.

So she knew! Jessica's mother had known there were others but Tess and Carla hadn't. So what about her own parents, where did they fit into all this? How much did they know? Did it even matter any more? It felt as if her life was over, as if it had never even existed, like nothing was real, like this was all an extension of her freaky dream. If only – if only that could be true!

'You have to go,' the woman said, talking quickly but loud enough for everyone to hear. 'I don't know what you're doing here or how you found us or what you want but you have to go. Please – Jessie mustn't know, she mustn't see you.'

'I think it's too late,' said Louise, as the front door of number 15 burst open and a girl came out, followed by a woman.

Dr Jay! What was she doing here? Louise found

her eyes flitting everywhere, watching Cate and her parents, watching Dr Jay, as she stopped just inside the gate, watching Jessica who'd already come out onto the street. Jessica was close enough now for Louise to see her face; her blue eyes, which looked huge, wide, the pupils large, seeming to grow darker, larger as she looked at Louise and Cate.

'Jessie, go back inside,' Louise heard Jessica's mother say.

Louise was aware of other people talking too and she could hear someone crying, perhaps more than one, but her attention was now fixed on Jessica, who'd ignored her mum's instruction. Louise could almost trace Jessica's thoughts. The confusion, the disbelief, all the tangled ideas that had flashed through her own mind when she'd first seen Cate, were clear in Jessica's oh-so-familiar face.

Louise waited for the screams, the hysterics that would surely follow but they didn't. Instead Jessica started to smile. It was a smile Louise recognized. She'd seen it in pictures of herself when she was collecting a swimming trophy or posing with the volleyball team after a win but it was a smile that looked totally out of place here.

'Jessie?' Louise heard Jessica's mother breathe. 'Jessie, I'm so sorry.'

Louise wasn't sure whether Jessica had heard her mother; she certainly didn't respond.

'Oh God, this is amazing,' said Jessica, still smiling, moving towards Cate, stretching out her hand, lightly touching Cate's face.

'Hey,' said Cate, stepping away.

Jessica had everyone's attention now. She was standing, more or less in the middle of the group, turning slowly to face Dr Jay who'd just ventured out onto the street.

'Granddad did this, didn't he?' Jessica asked. 'This is what you were trying to tell me, this is what everyone's been hiding. O-mi-god, this is just amazing. It's fantastic! I can't believe it! I can't believe you've kept it secret.'

Several people started to speak at once but it was Cate's voice that rose above the rest.

'Are you frigging mad or on drugs or what?' Cate yelled at Jessica. 'Or has *she* been brainwashing you?' Cate added, stabbing a finger in the direction of Dr Jay. 'Don't you get it, Jessica, are you completely thick? Don't you understand what they've done? Look at me! We're clones, we're freaks, we're bloody sideshow freaks and you think that's fantastic, do you?'

As Cate's voice rose ever higher, the door of

number 17 opened. An elderly woman stood on the doorstep, leaning on a walking stick, peering at them, shaking her head and Louise couldn't help hoping she was short-sighted as well as slightly infirm.

'Let's go inside, we need to go inside,' Jessica's mother said, herding them all forward, through the open gate.

12

Cate and Jessica were still shouting at each other,
Carla was yelling at Dr Jay and Tess was crying
but somehow Jessica's mum had managed to usher
them all inside into a small lounge. She even
managed to persuade some of them to sit down.
Louise didn't need any persuading. She slumped in
an armchair and seconds later Cate came and
perched on the arm beside her, like they were
suddenly allies, best mates.

Iain sat in the armchair opposite, looking as if
he wished he'd never got into any of this. Well, at
least he'd had some sort of choice and could walk
away any time he chose but what about them?
What about her parents, how much did they know,
would they get into trouble, go to prison even for
whatever part they'd played?

Tess had sat down on the sofa next to Jessica.
Carla took the only remaining seat, a small chair

in the corner, whilst Dr Jay and Jessica's mum remained standing. Somehow, amidst all the seat-choosing, the noise had settled so that now there was only Cate and Jessica hurling comments at each other.

'Don't you get it,' Jessica was saying, 'don't you realize how special this makes us? We're not freaks, we're incredible, we're unique.'

'Unique?' said Cate. 'You're kidding me, right? There are three of us, you moron! Three identical frigging clones, how can we be unique? There might even be more of us. They probably made a whole bloody batch.'

'Alex and Ben,' said Jessica, suddenly sitting up straight and looking at her mother, 'are they cloned too?'

'Good lord, no,' her mother said, 'they're just twins, ordinary twins, natural.'

She flushed as she said it.

'As opposed to unnatural?' said Cate, almost spitting the words across the room.

'So we really are the first?' said Jessica. 'The only ones?'

She was mad, as mad as Dr Jay!

'As far as I know,' said Dr Jay, 'yes, you're the only ones.'

'Unless there've been other secret projects,' said Cate, standing up. 'What's to say the Americans or the Koreans or the French haven't had a go, other bloody lunatics, all over the friggin' world, wanting to play God.'

'That was never what it was about,' said Dr Jay, leaning against the far wall, as if she was trying to disappear into it.

Louise wished she would. She wished they'd all disappear.

'What then?' said Cate. 'Why did you do it? Because you could, because it was possible, because you couldn't bloody resist, because you didn't care what it would mean, how we'd feel?'

'No,' said Dr Jay. 'It wasn't really even my field. I was a fertility specialist. I'd met Jessica's granddad, of course, collaborated on a couple of things.'

'You certainly did,' Jessica's mother murmured.

The words were loaded with a meaning Louise couldn't quite work out and wasn't even sure if she wanted to.

'I knew all about his work,' Dr Jay went on, stressing the word 'work' and looking towards Jessica. 'I knew what was possible theoretically, but it wasn't planned. It honestly wasn't planned. Then when Katherine was killed and I raised the possibility that we might . . . Your granddad didn't want to at first but, in the end he couldn't resist. Someone would have done it sooner or later and Katherine's DNA sample was perfect. I'd made sure of that.'

The mention of Katherine had cut through Louise's numbness, forcing memories, images out of the blackness, which made her start to shake, a violent trembling she couldn't control. Cate somehow noticed, even though she was half-turned away from Louise. She came to perch on the arm of the chair again, put her hand down to touch Louise's arm, like she actually cared. Her hand felt strangely cold in the suffocating heat of the room.

'You know about Katherine?' Dr Jay said, looking at Cate and Louise.

Louise couldn't answer and Cate, apparently, didn't want to because she looked down at the floor, as if studying the brownish flecks in the beige carpet.

'We know she was murdered,' said Iain, a little uncertainly, 'we know she was Tess and Carla's friend.'

'Was she that important?' Cate said, suddenly looking up towards Tess. 'Was she that bloody special that you couldn't let go, that you had to have her cloned like those freaks do with their dead spaniels? Let's raid the morgue and turn our dead friend into a nice new baby! Do you know how sick that is?'

'It wasn't like that,' Dr Jay said, moving towards the centre of the room. 'Katherine *was* special, incredibly special, and she wasn't just Tess and Carla's friend.'

'She was your sister, wasn't she,' Jessica said, 'your half-sister, the one you were telling me about?'

Louise felt the sickness gush into her throat again and fought to push it back. She'd known, she'd always felt that there was some connection, some personal connection to Dr Jay.

'It was so random,' Dr Jay was saying, 'so utterly random and pointless. Some lunatic, who'd attacked people before, let out early! Katherine should never have died like that. She was so young, so talented, it wasn't right, it wasn't fair.'

'Fair,' said Cate, 'and you think this is fair, do you? Did it work, did you get her back? Am I your precious bloody sister, is Louise or Jessica? Or are there others? How many did you clone to make sure you got at least one perfect bloody replica?'

'That's it though,' said Jessica, 'we're not Katherine, are wc? We're us. I don't really know you two but I can see how different we are! Don't you see what this could mean, what it could tell us, what it could prove?'

'Yeah,' said Cate, jabbing her finger towards Dr Jay, 'it proves she should be locked up, strung up!'

'Don't worry,' said Dr Jay, 'I probably will be when this gets out.'

The tightness clutched at Louise's throat again. Who else would be implicated? There must have been other scientists involved and what about her parents, Cate's parents and Jessica's mum?

'Good,' said Cate. 'But before they lock you up are you gonna answer my question – are there others?'

'We only implanted four,' Dr Jay said, her voice flat, 'and one of them miscarried.'

The shivering, which had settled a bit, started up again and Louise felt Cate's icy fingers squeezing her arm. They only implanted four so how many did they make, how many did they discard? How many possible Jessicas or Cates were thrown away and at what stage? How did they choose? What gave them the bloody right to do it at all?

'But we didn't know,' Carla was saying. 'Tell Cate we didn't know,' she added, looking towards Dr Jay.

'You knew enough,' Dr Jay said, 'and you agreed, nobody forced you, you wanted to do it.'

'And what about Louise's parents?' said Cate. 'Why did *they* do it? Were they that bloody desperate for a baby?'

'We chose all our parents carefully,' said Dr Jay. 'Although,' she added, looking at Jessica again, 'in one case not quite carefully enough. But Louise – well, yes, they were desperate, I suppose. Her parents had been to me for fertility treatment. And her mother had done some legal work for Jessica's granddad. We knew they'd be discreet, we could trust them.'

Louise moved Cate's hand, which was still holding her arm, and stood up. She didn't want to hear all this from Dr Jay; she didn't want to sit in this room full of people, analysing, arguing. She needed to hear it from her parents, or the people she'd always believed were her parents. She felt ill, she needed to go home. Cate had stood up too.

'Iain could take you,' Cate said, as if she had read her thoughts, like they were totally in tune. 'Do you want me to come with you?'

Louise shook her head. Strangely she wanted Cate around, wanted Cate to go back with her

219

but Cate needed to be here with Tess and Carla. Besides, Cate would want to stay until she'd rooted out all the details, all the answers from Dr Jay. Cate wouldn't walk away now.

'What's going to happen,' Louise said, 'to us, to her?' she added, looking at Dr Jay. 'We don't need to tell anyone, do we?' she added with sudden hope. 'There's no reason to tell, we could still keep it secret.'

'That's not an option, Lou,' Cate said, the hard edginess back in her voice, 'but we'll be OK. We'll have to be, won't we? Maybe we'll hire a publicist, be celebs instead of freaks, eh? Go to the press ourselves, make a bit of money out of this? What do you reckon, Lou?'

Louise couldn't answer because Cate was hugging her, squeezing her tight. Was Cate joking or would she really go down that route? She could imagine Cate in the spotlight, making out like being a clone was the best thing in the world, but not her. She just wanted to hide away, pretend it wasn't happening. She wasn't like Cate. She kept those words lodged at the front of her mind as she prepared to leave. She wasn't like Cate or Jessica or even Katherine; she was Louise, she was herself – she was still the same person she'd always been

– no one could take that away from her, could they?

Jessica sat in the lounge with Mum long after the others had gone, after Dr Jay had volunteered to go to the police, after Cate's family had insisted on going with her, to make sure she didn't escape!

'I'm sorry. I'm so sorry, Jessie,' Mum had kept saying over and over, which was crazy because Mum was the least to blame, if there was any question of blame at all.

All Mum had been told, at first, was the abandoned baby story – the story that had fooled social services, the police and the adoption courts; the story that Ben and Alex, all their wider family, all their friends, still believed to be true. Granddad had been so careful, so clever about all that. The cover story was meticulous, as Dr Jay had pointed out, convincing in every detail.

Later, when Mum had totally bonded with baby Jessica, when there was no chance of letting go, giving her up, Granddad had confessed – in part. Sure baby Jessica had been abandoned, in a way, only not at a bus stop. The not-so-carefully-chosen surrogate parents had second thoughts. They didn't want a cloned baby after all. It was too creepy, too unnatural. They'd agreed to keep quiet but they didn't want her.

'Your granddad started to have second thoughts almost immediately,' Dr Jay had said.

Well yeah, he might have done but it had taken six years or so before he eventually cracked, told Dad the full truth about the others; about Cate and Louise and the one that had miscarried. Then in the early hours of the following morning he'd died. So maybe the overdose wasn't accidental after all. Dr Jay had hinted as much – his constant guilt, his remorse. Oh God, it was so, so stupid. Jessica shook her head. This was the hardest part – thinking of the things that should never have happened, the results of all the secrets and lies. It was all so pointless, so utterly bloody pointless.

She looked at her com, which was switched off. Kal had been trying to get in touch but she couldn't face talking to him just yet. She'd tell him, of course, just not now. It was hardly the sort of thing you could just blurt out over the phone the day before his brother's wedding! Besides she had other people to talk to first.

Dad hadn't told Mum about what had gone on with him and Granddad at the time. She wasn't sure why. The result of guilt, grief and the fear at how Mum might react – knowing how badly *he'd* reacted and what it had led to. But it was a big, big mistake because when he'd been forced to tell Mum she'd flipped completely. So priority was talking to Dad. Yeah, she could ask him, get his side of the story, try to fill in some of the gaps. Mum wouldn't stop her any more. There was no point.

'It was when you saw that girl at the Science Museum that I first started to wonder,' Mum had said. 'It was just a vague suspicion at first, with all the talk of doubles and twins. I thought I was being paranoid but the minute I asked your dad I knew he was lying. I knew what they'd done!'

Trouble was, Mum believed he'd always been lying, that he'd known everything from the start, that he was part of the conspiracy with Granddad and Dr Jay. Maybe part of Mum believed that still, even after everything Dr Jay had said. Jessica looked over at Mum who still looked exhausted.

'I was only ever trying to protect you,' Mum said, as she'd said a dozen times before.

'I know,' said Jessica.

What else could she say? Poor Mum! She'd only ever done what she thought was right. She just hadn't realized there was nothing to protect.

'I shouldn't have kept you away from your dad,' Mum said, her voice heavy. 'I was just so angry. Maybe we should all have been more honest, more open from the start.'

'We can't change what's happened, Mum,' she said, moving across the room to sit beside her. 'We need to look forward – work out what to do next. We need to tell people – the people who matter – before they read about it in the papers!'

'How?' said her mother. 'How do we even start?'

Jessica wasn't sure but Ben, Alex, all their family and friends would have to be told.

'What are people going to say?' her mum added.

Jessica wondered whether she was thinking of Jonathon. Would he still want to marry her, would he mind being step-father to a freak! From Mum's relationship, Jessica's mind flashed to her own; to her and Kal. She stood up, turned on her com and walked over to the window. She'd have to answer his texts, at least, or he'd start worrying. She really ought to tell him soon anyway because if bloody Cate had her way it could be all over the news by the end of the day!

'We need to start now,' she told Mum, filled with a sudden urgency. 'I'll try and get Ben and Alex on video-link.'

Her mum nodded but made no attempt to move. Clearly Mum wasn't going to be much help for a while so she'd have to tell the twins herself – once she'd worked out what she was going to say. Surely it couldn't make any difference to anything, not really, not to anyone with half a brain. She was still the same Jessica. No way was she going to start acting apologetic or ashamed or anything, not to the boys or Kal or anyone!

In a funny way it was easier to accept being a clone than being abandoned, she reflected as she headed upstairs. At least this way she was sure of her roots and being cloned wasn't so very different from being born the more normal way. She'd taken the raw material Granddad and Dr Jay had given her, moulded it, made it her own, become Jessica. And there was nothing, as far she could see, absolutely nothing wrong with that.

Cate closed the curtains, shutting out the mass of reporters and photographers who'd been swarming at the gate for the past two days. From the moment they'd got back home, the bloody reporters had been there. They'd only let one of them in. Exclusive interview – that was the deal. Jessica, bless her, was planning to give it all out for free eventually. Jessica, apparently, was going to talk to the scientific magazines, wave the flag for science and progress, stick to the facts.

Well good for her but most people weren't interested in how it had been done. They didn't care about all the oh-so-clever techniques or what it might prove about genes. Most people wanted the human angle, the gossip, the scandal. They wanted to know about Katherine, Dr Jay and how it felt to be a clone.

Well sure, she could give them all the stupid rubbish they wanted – for a price. And a very good price she'd been promised too! Louise had taken a different approach – her choice, of course, but totally the wrong one. If you couldn't change things, couldn't even begin to come to terms with it, which she couldn't, then you might as well exploit it. There'd already been talk of a modelling contract, a documentary, a Hollywood film, her own chat show even – but first the interview.

The reporter was already settled, pen poised, voice recorder set up on the coffee table. Top guy they'd sent who looked a bit like a bulldog. He acted like one too, the way he'd barged his way through the rest of the press pack. He must be well used to interviewing celebrities but she could see he was keyed-up by this one, imagining the story on the front page, the centre spread and probably most of the pages in between. He was so excited he was almost slavering. Gross! Well he'd have to wait. Marcus, the publicist they'd hired, was still upstairs with Tess and Carla, raiding the computers and digi-frames for photos tracking her life.

'Don't start the interview without me,' Marcus had said.

Stupid really, she could cope with bulldog man. OK, so she'd have to be careful. There was stuff she'd promised not to tell, like how they'd first found out about Katherine. She'd promised Louise she wouldn't mention the nightmares. Not that anyone would believe it. You honestly couldn't make it up!

They hadn't got around to asking Jessica if she had the nightmares too. She wasn't even sure she wanted to know. It would all come out in time though, especially if they were rounded up to face doctors and psychologists, wired up to dream-monitoring machines, turned into little lab rats. And they would be, if they weren't careful!

For now though, she'd promised to keep Lou out of it as much as possible. Bulldog man would want something on Louise, of course. He'd want to know how alike they were, whether they got on, that sort of crap. She wanted to steer clear of too much talk about Tess and Carla too, but people were just gonna love that angle, weren't they? Marcus was pressing them to do their own deal, tell their own story.

There was a limit, apparently, to what the papers could say about Dr Jay. Facts, according to Marcus, would have to be checked and treble-checked in case Dr Jay decided to challenge any of it, sue the paper. Not that she would. She was playing the heroine now, accepting full responsibility.

As far as Dr Jay was concerned, persuading Jessica's granddad to do the deed was the high spot of her bloody life. After that she'd quit her job, changed her name, more than once, moved abroad and kept a low profile working as a nurse in various clinics, old people's homes and hospices; temporary contracts to earn money to fuel her main obsession – the monitoring of her and Louise.

'I cared about you, you know,' she'd said.

Well maybe she did in her own weird, twisted sort of way. But it was still sick. Jessica's mum had known. That's why she'd kept her away from Jessica, unmoved by Dr Jay's claims that the checkups had to be done in case complications set in.

Complications basically meant early death – a little side effect that had plagued the early experiments with animals.

That's why Tess, Carla and Louise's parents had agreed but Cate still couldn't get her head round why they'd accepted a cloned baby in the first place. She probably never would, unless she ever got that desperate for a kid herself – and she might, one day – because a lot of cloned animals had turned out to be infertile. Nature's way of fighting back! She looked up as her parents came in with Marcus. Bulldog man looked up too.

'Right,' he said, 'excellent. No need to be nervous, Cate. What we want is the story in your own words, OK. Are you ready?'

He barely gave her time to answer before the machine was switched on but mainly he did what he said and let her tell it in her own way with just the occasional question or prompt. The only tricky bit came at the end when the recorder had been switched off and they started talking about pictures.

'Those are great,' the reporter had said, checking the ones on offer, 'but what we really need is one of the three girls together.'

'Yeah, well that's not very likely,' Cate told him.

'We think Jessica might,' the reporter said,

'with the right sort of approach. But no one's been able to find Louise, of course. You wouldn't happen to . . .'

'No,' said Cate, 'no idea.'

'Not to worry,' he said, 'we'll find her eventually but there's a considerable sum on offer if we could find her sooner rather than later.'

'Bloody hell!' said Cate, when he named a figure. 'You are desperate! And don't worry, if she gets in touch, you'll be the first to know.'

She let Marcus show the reporter out, went up to her room and picked up her phone. Louise's self-appointed guardian angel answered.

'Hi, Iain,' Cate said, 'is she there?'

Obviously she was; she didn't dare move! God knows how long she was going to hide herself away in the bolt-hole Iain had found for her and her parents. No doubt she'd crawl out eventually, face the world but, in the meantime, Louise's secret was safe with her.

Louise stared at the ever-growing pile of newspapers on the small kitchen table. The house Iain had found was great, far more remote than the places Dr Jay used to choose for her check-ups. They'd thought about going abroad at first but Iain had said they'd never get out of the country and besides, he knew just the place. And so far it had worked; no one had bothered them.

She'd had the time, the space she wanted to talk with her parents – not that it had helped, not that she was any nearer to understanding. But at least, like Tess and Carla, they'd believed she was the only one and they'd seemed almost relieved that the secret had finally come out. Strangely, it hadn't really changed her relationship with her parents. You didn't stop loving your family just because they'd made mistakes, screwed up your life, or even because you didn't share their genes.

She spread the papers out a bit, looking at some of the headlines, the editorials and centre page spreads. It had been more than a fortnight since the story broke but people couldn't get enough, it seemed. The radio and TV were full of it, whole sites had appeared on the net and the papers talked about nothing else.

EXCLUSIVE – How I Found my Clone Sisters. Good old Cate! She could see Cate almost every day on some TV programme or other, Jessica too sometimes. Jessica serious, Cate laughing, joking and playing to the cameras. You'd have to know Cate well to see the anger in her eyes.

And, on the letters page, readers' letters full of condemnation, admiration, pity. Everybody had a view, everybody wanted their say.

Girls Cloned to 'Replace' Dead Sister. That was the article that really freaked her, the one that majored on Katherine, spilling out all the details of her life, her tragic death at the age of twenty-four. It wasn't so much an article as a biography, filling almost every page of the paper with pictures of Katherine alongside pictures of Cate, scary comparisons about IQ, all the statistics, all the similarities.

She'd read it over and over checking which parts of Katherine were strong in her, which characteristics Cate had 'inherited' and which were more obvious in Jessica. Same genes, different people, like Cate had said, how weird was that? Sensitivity in Katherine had mutated into neurosis in her; Katherine's determination had become ferocity in Cate. She didn't know Jessica well enough to be sure but, from what she could tell, Jessica was most like the original.

Police Investigate Clone Claims. This was a less sensational piece in a serious paper, all about the complexities of the law and the case against Dr Jay that could take years to get to court. The police still wanted to talk to her parents but it seemed that there'd be no charges against them. Cate's parents hadn't been charged or Jessica's – or at least not yet.

U.S. Clone Claim Hoax. How mad was that? Twenty-five year old American triplets trying to make out they were cloned, that they were the first. And they weren't the only ones. There'd been dozens of claims already. With any luck some would turn out to be true, take the focus away from them. She threw the newspaper onto the floor, with the others she'd discarded and stared at the next headline.

Clone Girl Hunt. That was her they were talking about! Hunt, for heaven's sake! As if she was a dangerous animal to be rounded up and shot. There were pleas for her to come forward. Psychologists were claiming she'd need help, counselling. Well, they were probably right about that but no way was she going within a million miles of any sort of doctor.

She'd have to surface sometime though. There was poor Aunt Mary to think about, for a start. She'd had to go into temporary care and the cats were languishing in a cattery. Iain had arranged all that for them but Iain couldn't look after them for ever, he had his own life to lead – just like she had.

'Get a grip, Lou,' Cate had said, the last time she'd phoned. 'It's still your own life, for heaven's sake, take control.'

Well she would take control. She was! Over the last week she'd started to eat properly again, she was managing a few hours' sleep each night and, strangely, she hadn't had the nightmare. It was time to move on. OK, maybe not today or tomorrow but soon. She stood up and looked out to where her parents were sitting in the very private garden.

It was funny, in some ways she felt just like she'd always done, like nothing had changed but, of course, it had, totally, forever and for everyone. They were the first human clones and, although they probably wouldn't be the last, they'd always be special. The names Cate, Jessica, Louise would forever be associated with clones.

It's still your own life, Cate had said but she was wrong. When she finally came out of hiding, her life would never entirely be her own. Could she cope with that? The answer had to be yes. She wasn't quite sure how but somehow, some way, in her own way, she'd manage.